Ministry Between Miracles

Caring for Hurting People in the Power of the Holy Spirit

THOMSON K. MATHEW

Library of Congress Control Number: 2002113252
ISBN 1-591603-76-5

Xulon Press
11350 Random Hills Road
Suite 800
Fairfax, VA 22030
(703) 279-6511
XulonPress.com

To order additional copies, call 1-866-909-BOOK (2665).

This book is dedicated to
my father and first pastor,
K. Thomas Mathew

Contents

Author's Perspective

My hope is that this work will help Spirit-filled pastors and counselors become better trained to care for hurting people in the power of the Holy Spirit.

There is a worldwide shortage of listeners and a surplus of talkers. Anyone who can listen with support, care and empathy adds great value to our lives. The human need to be heard is universal; unfortunately, the ability to listen is not as pervasive as the need to be listened to. Listening skills must be learned through concentration and much practice.

Christian caregiving is accurate communication of God's love; psychology is one of the tools that can help the person hear that message of love.

God cares, and God will bring comfort, reconciliation, restoration, and healing.

Thomson K. Mathew

Foreword

The history of pastoral care is a long one. Originally known as "the cure of souls," it is as old as the Wisdom literature contained in the Proverbs and Ecclesiastes.

The literature of pastoral care in also theologically diverse. This literature may be found in most major faith groups, including theistic and non-theistic religions. Varying theological perspectives differ in the roles ascribed and attributed to God, to the person in need of care, or to naturally occurring circumstances and events. These perspectives are intended to enhance one's understanding of the circumstances and situations necessitating care as well as to direct caregiving activities.

In this regard, the field of pastoral care involved wide-ranging techniques that arise from varying (and often opposing) approaches to psychology, medicine, and religious practice. Mental imagery and non-directive counseling techniques such as acceptance and listening co-exist with more insight-oriented approaches that are intended to help persons "understand" themselves. Prayer and scripture are used, at times, in conjunction with medication and the use of physicians. At other times prayer and scripture are used as prescriptions in their own right.

What has been missing from this extensive conversation until now is an approach to pastoral care that is fully oriented toward the Spirit-life traditions: expressions of Trinitarian Christianity that acknowledge God as the source of life, living, health and wholeness, the salvific benefits of Christ, and the comforting presence and direction of the Holy Spirit. This book, based on the author's extensive experience as the pastor of a large Pentecostal church in New England, as a chaplain who was responsible for praying for persons who were themselves "faith-healers," and as a seminary professor at the oldest and largest Pentecostal/Charismatic seminary in the world, fills that gap. It provides a balanced perspective of personal faith as well as specific personal characteristics and activities necessary for a successful ministry of caring. It integrated pastoral care concepts suggested by theologians old and new with those of psychologists, pastors, and chaplains. The result is a truly unique perspective of pastoral care.

Edward E. Decker, Jr., Ph.D.
Professor, Christian Counseling
School of Theology and Missions
Oral Roberts University

Introduction

With the arrival of the new millennium, the modern Pentecostal movement is about to celebrate its centennial. After a hundred years of ministry emphasizing the salvation of souls, many in the charismatic/Pentecostal movement are appreciating the importance of caring for these souls.

In order to strengthen the caregiving ministries in Pentecostal and charismatic circles, caregivers in these ministries have been communicating among themselves and have formed the Fellowship of Pentecostal/Charismatic Caregivers (FPCC). The FPCC conferences and publications are doing much to enhance the ministry of "Spirit-led pastoral care" in full gospel churches and ministries. However, there is still a significant lack of written materials for use by practitioners and teachers of Spirit-led pastoral care.

There is no way one author or school could meet the acute need for academic materials written from a Pentecostal/charismatic perspective on the subject of pastoral care. These pages represent my contribution toward meeting this challenge. All of us—practitioners, professors, and students of Spirit-led pastoral care—will need to share our growing body of knowledge with one another.

I begin with a review of the history of Pentecostal pastoral care. Chapter 2 develops a Pentecostal theology of pastoral ministry. I admit that it is a personal theology based on reflections on my own educational and practical experiences. In chapters 3 and 4, I attempt to analyze the concept of caring and present one way of dealing with the psychological side of caregiving. Chapter 5 deals with assessment.

Chapter 6 presents a simple model of care ministry that can be implemented in clinical contexts as well as in the local church. Because caregivers cannot escape encounter with suffering, Chapter 7 is devoted to a pastoral understanding of the problem of suffering.

This monograph concludes with a Gospel-based Pentecostal model of caregiving: a model that sees pastoral care as a ministry between miracles. I believe this model is faithful to the Word and the Spirit.

This is a work in progress. Some things in it will no doubt be changed as I reflect further on this aspect of God's work in the world and receive input from readers who can add to the thoughts and experiences presented here. I am grateful to all the people who have invested in my life, beginning with my first pastor--my own father. I am also grateful to my students, who have taught me much. As a third-generation Pentecostal minister, I long for a revival that will balance soul-saving and soul care. I desire so much to take part in such a move of God. If these pages generate meaningful discussion about Pentecostal/charismatic pastoral care as it relates to God's overall plan of salvation, wholeness and redemption, I will consider myself greatly rewarded.

I want to express my gratitude to Ruth McIntosh for extensive editorial and typesetting assistance with this manuscript.

Thomson K. Mathew, D.Min., Ed.D.
Dean, School of Theology and Missions
Oral Roberts University
Tulsa, Oklahoma

Summer 2002

1

History of Spirit-Led Pastoral Care

The history of pastoral care[1] begins with God the Heavenly Shepherd. David the Psalmist sang about the Shepherd God in the 23rd Psalm. The Apostle Paul described God as "the Father of compassion and the God of all comfort ..." (2 Cor 1:3), whose caring nature revealed itself to humanity in his Son, Jesus Christ. The history of pastoral care continues in the story of the ministry of Jesus of Nazareth.

Old and New Testaments

The Old Testament describes the shepherding ministry of prophets and priests who were servants of the Shepherd God.

---

1   A slightly different version of this chapter was published in John K. Vining, ed., *The Spirit of the Lord Is Upon Me: Essential Papers on Spirit-Filled Caregiving* (East Rockaway, NY: Cummings and Hathaway Publishers, 1997).

The New Testament presents Jesus Christ as the Great Shepherd of the new covenant who gives up his life for the sheep. He appoints apostles, prophets, evangelists, pastors and teachers to continue his work of perfecting the saints. The pastor-teachers are to lead (Acts 20:28-31), guide (1 Pet 2:25), instruct (1 Tim 2:7), and correct (1 Cor 12:28-29) the people of God. They are instructed to feed (1 Pet 5:2), edify (2 Cor 13:10), build up (Eph 4:12), comfort (2 Cor 1:3-4), rebuke (Titus 1:13), warn (Acts 20: 31), and watch for souls (Heb 13:17).

Charles Ver Straten sees the connection between the Old and New Testaments in this regard and points out that Jesus the Good Shepherd intentionally trained his apostles to do the work of the ministry. Jesus ordained his disciples so that they could preach, teach, heal and drive out demons (Mt 9:36-38, Mk 3:14, 15; 6:13), but New Testament ministry was much more than performance. Pastoral ministry in the New Testament was a ministry of the heart. This ministry of the heart is evident in the fact that while the Jewish elders functioned as administrators, the Christian elders *(presbyteros)* functioned like shepherds.[2]

Major Themes in the Church Fathers

The Shepherd

It appears that the 2nd Century Church viewed the bishop as the successor of the apostle. While this was a deviation from the practice of the primitive church, it emphasizes the importance the early church gave to pastoral work and ministry. The pastoral concern of the early church is seen in Polycarp's description of the qualifications of a presbyter: "[They] must be compassionate, merciful towards all men, turning back the sheep that are gone

---

2   Charles A. Ver Straten, *A Caring Church* (Grand Rapids: Baker, 1988), 146.

astray, visiting all the infirm, not neglecting a widow or an orphan or a poor man."[3]

The writings of the church fathers give clear evidence of the strong position of pastoral care in the ministry of the developing church. Both the person of the caregiver and the caregiving method received their attention. Thomas Oden has done a great service by providing a collection of these writings in his *Classical Pastoral Care* series.[4] Gregory the Great wanted each pastor to be a person who "out of affection of heart sympathizes with another's infirmity."[5]

The Trained Pastor

John Chrysostom emphasized the importance of training for pastoral caregivers: "Anyone who is about to enter upon this ministry needs to explore it all thoroughly beforehand and only then to undertake this ministry. And why? Because if he studies the difficulties beforehand he will at any rate have the advantage of not being taken by surprise when they crop up."[6]

The shepherding metaphor is strong in the writing of early fathers. "The Good Shepherd makes it His business to seek for the best pastures for His sheep, and to find green and shady groves where they may rest during the noonday heat," says Origen.[7] "Therefore, dearly beloved Brother, take heed that the undisciplined be not consumed and perish, that you rule the brotherhood as far as possible with salutary counsels, and that you counsel each one for his salvation," advised Cyprian.[8] Chrysostom saw shepherding as an awesome responsibility. He made sure that the limits of the shepherding metaphor were not ignored: "You cannot treat human beings with the same authority

---

3 James F. Stitzinger, "Pastoral Ministry in History," in *Rediscovering Pastoral Ministry,* edited by John A. MacArthur, Jr. (Dallas: Word, 1995), 42.

4 Thomas C. Oden, *Classical Pastoral Care*, vols. 1-4, (Grand Rapids: Baker, 1987-94).

5 Oden, *Classical Pastoral Care*, vol. 1, 12.

6 Ibid., 13.

7 Ibid., 41.

8 Ibid., 42.

with which the shepherd treats a sheep. Here too is possible to bind and to forbid food and to apply cautery and the knife, but the decision to receive treatment does not lie with the one who administers the medicine but actually with the patient."[9]

The need for preparation for pastoral work is described in the writings of Origen and Tertullian. Origen compared learning of secular subjects by priests to the spoiling of the Egyptians by the Israelites: "How useful to the children of Israel were the things brought from Egypt, which the Egyptians had not put to a proper use, but which the Hebrews, guided by the wisdom of God, used for God's service?"[10] Tertullian did appreciate the need for acquiring secular knowledge for polemic reasons, but he cautioned against uncritical reliance on secular knowledge for the work of the ministry. "What indeed has Athens to do with Jerusalem? What concord is there between the Academy and the Church? What between heretics and the Christians? Our instruction comes from 'the porch of Solomon' who himself wrote: 'Set your mind upon the Lord, as is your duty, and seek him with simplicity of heart' (Wisdom of Solomon 1:1). Away with all attempts to produce a mottled Christianity of Stoic, Platonic, and dialectic composition.[11]

Ministerial self-awareness and congruence were important to early fathers. "You cannot put straight in others what is warped in yourself," said Athanasius.[12] Black Moses, a 3rd Century African ascetic, said: "If a man's deeds are not in harmony with his prayer, he labours in vain. The brother said, 'What is this harmony between practice and prayer?' The old man said, 'We should no longer do those things against which we pray.'"[13] Gregory the Great wrote, "While he is obliged to speak what is good to those under his charge, he must first observe matters of which he speaks."[14]

---

9   Ibid., 43.
10 Ibid., 169.
11 Ibid., 170.
12 Ibid., 174.
13 Ibid., 175.
14 Ibid.

Pastoral Duties

Pastoral care in the early church gave priority to the resources of the church, such as Word, prayer, and sacraments. The Word of God was seen as central to the care of souls. Pastoral prayer held a very high place in ministering to people. The sacraments of baptism and communion served as noble instruments of care.

Teaching was an important ministry of the caregivers of the early church. The assumption was that through teaching the Word, one can guide souls toward higher levels of virtue. Clement of Alexandria[15] and Athanasius[16] wrote on the pedagogical aspects of ministry. Jesus was their model teacher. They noted that he also embodied his own teachings.

Supportive Community

The community of faith was an important resource in the care of souls. The church as the body of Christ was not only the context of caregiving, but it was also a participant in that ministry. In addition to being the sacramental community of healing, the congregation became a provider of care by financially supporting the needy among them as well as the priestly caregivers.

Reconciler

Reconciliation was a major theme of pastoral work in the early church. Polycarp, Bishop of Smyrna, wrote about his approach to dealing with a fallen clergy. "You too, for your part, must not be over severe with them, for people of that kind are not to be looked on as enemies; you have to restore them, like parts of your own person that are ailing and going wrong, so that the whole body can be maintained in health. Do this, and you will be promoting your own spiritual welfare at the same time."[17]

Counseling was a major part of pastoral care in the early church. Empathy was seen as a very important ingredient of

---

15　Oden, *Classical Pastoral Care*, vol. 3, 72-73.
16　Oden, *Classical Pastoral Care*, vol. 2, 178.
17　Ibid., 223.

good soul care. Several images of the counselor can be seen in the early writings. The caregiver is a physician bringing healing to people. He is a guide to those who are on a journey. He sets people free from bondages, and teaches them like a faithful educator.[18] To summarize the earliest form of a theology of caregiving: God is the original caregiver, who initiated the ministry of caregiving. We learn this ministry from his Son. The care one gives is a reflection of the care of God. The Holy Spirit is the best Counselor. We are led by the Spirit in our ministry of counseling. "In the case of the Holy Spirit, the Paraclete must be understood in the sense of comforter, inasmuch as He bestows consolation upon the souls to whom He openly reveals the apprehension of spiritual knowledge," said Origen.[19]

Pastoral counseling and teaching should be fully based on the Word of God. Scripture provides the wisdom for counsel. According to Clement of Alexandria, "The inspired Word exists because of both obedience and disobedience: that we may be saved by obeying it, educated because we have disobeyed."[20] According to Origen, by studying the Word of God one becomes "a participator of all the doctrines of his counsel."[21]

The church fathers wrote about the methodological issues of counseling. They paid attention to the importance of silence, the use of language, and the reading of body language. For them, counseling was not value-free. Pastors were expected to give moral counseling. Scripture was to inform them in moral guidance.

The church fathers emphasized the importance of using one's words wisely. Careful attention must be given to the use of language in counseling and ministry. Ambrose wrote, "The Spirit of Wisdom described in the Book of Wisdom is subtle and lively, because in her is the spirit of understanding, holy, one, manifold,

---

18   Oden, *Classical Pastoral Care*, vol. 3, 52–76.
19   Ibid., 100.
20   Ibid., 104.
21   Ibid., 103.

lively; and she grinds her words before speaking so that she may not offend in any mode or meaning."[22]

Discerner

Spiritual discernment was also important to the church fathers. Pastoral counseling required spiritual discernment. One needed to be open to the Spirit and the Word to exercise proper discernment. Scriptural counsel had to be given with spiritual discernment.

According to Oden, the artificial separation of psychology, ethics and theology did not exist in classical pastoral care. A balance between the sternness of the law and the mercy of the gospel was maintained. The tension between guilt and forgiveness, grace and effort, discipline and freedom, and law and gospel were acknowledged by the early church.[23]

Therapist

Habit modification was a concern for earlier pastoral counselors. Oden points out that behavior modification is not a modern discovery. Earlier pastoral counselors documented the behavior of their counselees for the purpose of observing changes. They utilized special strategies to assist individuals to change their unhealthy behavior patterns.

Theologian

Crisis ministries were part of classical pastoral care. Many classical writers discussed the importance and methodologies of crisis intervention. Special emphasis was given to the care of the sick, especially the seriously sick. Efforts were made to offer the ministries of the church to the sick and dying.[24]

The issue of suffering was discussed in detail by early pastoral writers. Pastoral work required an honest encounter with the

---

22   Ibid., 138.
23   Ibid., 199.
24   Oden, *Classical Pastoral Care*, vol. 4, 3-25.

issue of suffering. Classical pastoral writers struggled with the issue of theodicy. The connection between evil and suffering was of considerable interest to early church fathers. Athanasius wrote, for instance, "The truth of the Church's theology must be manifest: that evil has not from the beginning been with God or in God, nor has [evil] any substantive existence; but that men, in default of the vision of good, began to devise and imagine for themselves what was not, after their own pleasure. For as if a man, when the sun is shining, and the whole earth illuminated by his light, were to shut fast his eyes and imagine darkness where no darkness exists, and then walk wandering as if in darkness, often falling and going down steep places, thinking it was dark and not light—for, imagining that he sees, he does not see at all—so, too, the soul of man, shutting fast her eyes, by which she is able to see God, has imagined evil for herself, and moving therein, knows not that, thinking she is doing something, she is doing nothing."[25]

Marriage Counselor

Pastoral care of marriage and family was a major concern of earlier caregivers. Much has been said by classical pastoral writers about the marriage covenant, the husband/wife relationship, sexuality and parenting. Marriage counseling is not a modern invention. The church has always been concerned about the well being of marriage and family life. Biblical advice and practical helps were provided by pastoral caregivers of the first centuries.[26]

Benefactor

Care of the poor and widows also received much attention. Instructions were given in the obligations of the church to the poor and needy. The care of the poor involved more than just offering pastoral support; it also included offering food, drink, shelter and clothing. Concerning the care of the poor, Ambrose said, "There is a two-fold liberality: one gives actual assistance,

---

25   Ibid., 63.
26   Ibid., 94-143.

that is, in money. The other is busy in offering help of more consequential and ennobling kind ... Money is easily spent. Good counsels can never be exhausted."[27]

Death and the process of dying have always been a major focus of pastoral care. Classical pastoral writers have written about the process and meaning of death, how to prepare people for dying, and how to minister to those who are left behind. Christian hope is at the center of such a ministry. Irenaeus put it most succinctly: "To die is to lose vital power, and to become henceforth breathless, inanimate, and devoid of motion, and to melt away into those [component parts] of [its] substance. But this event happens neither to the soul, for it is the breath of life, nor to the spirit, for the spirit is simple and not composite, so that it cannot be decomposed, and is itself the life of those who receive it."[28]

The writings of the church fathers teach us that pastoral care was a major ministry of the church during the early centuries. We are unable to claim that this was uniquely Pentecostal pastoral care; we can, however, claim that modern Spirit-led pastoral care is and should be connected to this rich tradition. Eddie Hyatt, on the other hand, sees a thread of charismatic ministry throughout the history of the church. In his book, *2000 Years of Charismatic Christianity*, Hyatt offers evidence in support of his claim. He presents Justin Martyr (A.D. 100-165), Irenaeus (125-200), Tertullian (160-240), Origen (185-284) and others among the ante-Nicene fathers to support his claim. Among the Monastics, he identifies Antony (251-356), Pachomius (292-346), Athanasius (295-373), Hilarion (305-385), Ambrose (340-397), Jerome (347-420), Augustine (354-430), Benedict (480-547), and Gregory the Great (540-604).[29]

---

27 Ibid., 149.
28 Ibid., 176.
29 Eddie Hyatt, Jr., *2000 Years of Charismatic Christianity* (Tulsa: Hyatt International Ministries, 1996).

Middle Ages and Pre-Reformation Period

Eddie Hyatt traces the history of the church through the "Dark Ages" to show that a charismatic tradition survived in spite of suppression and persecution, although often in history the tradition was seen more as part of various heresies. Although some of Hyatt's claims will be seriously challenged, one must admit that the ministry of healing did indeed survive those years. In that sense one can say also that a Pentecostal version of pastoral care also continued. However, I feel that without having to claim a Pentecostal/charismatic parallel to the "mainline" history of the church, modern Spirit-led Pentecostals and charismatics should trace their history through the major streams of the churches of the East and West.

Although the church of the Middle Ages became corrupted in many ways, pastoral care as spiritual direction flourished during this period, especially in the monastic tradition. A more biblical and classical pastoral care must have taken place among the Cathari (ca. 1050), Albigenses (1140), and Waldenses. The theological positions held by pre-Reformation reformers like John Wycliffe (1324-1384), John Huss (1373-1415) and William Tyndale (1494-1536) played an important role in keeping ministry biblical, as opposed to papal, and this must necessarily have included the practice of a more biblical form of pastoral care.

The Reformers

Pastoral care was a major concern of the Reformers. Martin Luther, John Calvin and Ulrich Zwingli found caregiving an important pastoral task.

Pastoral Study

Luther wrote about the importance of soul care and the preparation of ministers to provide such care: "Therefore I admonish you, especially those of you who are to become instructors of consciences, as well as each of you individually, that you exercise yourselves by study, by reading, by meditation, and by prayer, so that in temptation you will be able to instruct consciences, both your own and others,' console them, and take them from the Law to grace, from active righteousness to passive righteousness, in short, from Moses to Christ."[30] Although Luther believed in the priesthood of all believers, he placed the pastoral office in a more distinctive position. He considered the Scriptures the best textbook for pastors. Concerning the writings of the fathers, Luther said, "We are like men who study the signposts and never travel the road. The dear fathers wished, by their writings, to lead us to the Scriptures, but we so use them as to be led away from the Scriptures, though the Scriptures alone are our vineyard in which we ought all to work and toil."[31] Luther "put great emphasis on pastoral care, which always related directly to the ministry of the Word."[32]

Incarnational Presence

Luther believed in an incarnational approach to teaching and pastoral ministry. "When Christ wished to attract and instruct men," Luther said, "He had to become a man. If we are to attract and instruct children, we must become children with them."[33] Luther also believed in unconditional love as a condition for helping relationships. He believed that "there is no person on earth so bad that he does not have something about him that is praiseworthy."[34]

For Luther, pastoral care involved much more than teaching; it involved nurturing. "Therefore something more than merely preaching the Law is required, that a man may also know how he may be enabled to keep it. Otherwise what good does it do to preach that Moses and the Law merely say: This thou shalt do; this God requires of thee. Yes, my dear Moses, I hear what you say; and it is no doubt right and true. But do tell me where am I to get the ability to do what I have unfortunately not done and

---

30   Oden, *Classical Pastoral Care,* vol. 1, 149.
31   Ibid., 160.
32   Stitzinger, 52.
33   Oden, *Classical Pastoral Care,* vol. 2, 171.
34   Oden, *Classical Pastoral Care,* vol. 3, 28.

cannot do."[35] Soul care must involve enabling people to live the Christian life in a practical way. Anyone can share the "oughts"—it takes a caring pastor to help persons live the virtuous life.

Hope-Bearer

Luther understood the importance of having a theology of suffering. His own theology was built on Christian hope. He believed that "whatever hurts and distresses us does not happen to hurt or harm us but is for our good and profit. We must compare this to the work of the vinedresser who hoes and cultivates his vine."[36]

Luther had much to say about marriage, parenting and family life. He wrote much on being a good husband and wife and the responsibilities of parenting. Pastoral concern for the family was of utmost importance to him. He admonished husbands "to help, support, and protect her, not to harm her."[37]

Luther had a profound understanding of the grief process. His writings about the subject bring to mind more modern theories of death, dying and the grief process. Here again, Luther's pastoral ministry was guided by his theology of hope. He saw death as a journey from a world of misery and tears to a world of blessedness.

Servant and Protector

Calvin saw the ministry of caring as an aspect of the ministry of *diakonia* or service. The thrust of this ministry involved care of the poor and the sick. Calvin saw the ministry of pastor as proclaiming the Word, instructing, admonishing, private and public exhorting and censuring, and enjoining "brotherly corrections." Obviously, pastoral care and counseling were important aspects of the ministry as Calvin saw it. He believed that the pastor must do preaching, governing and pastoring. "A pastor

---

35   Ibid., 200.
36   Oden, *Classical Pastoral Care,* vol. 4, 71.
37   Ibid., 99.

needs two voices," he said, "one for gathering the sheep and the other for driving away wolves and thieves. Scripture supplies him with the means for doing both.[38]

Martin Bucer (1491-1551) was a disciple of Luther and a teacher of Calvin. According to James F. Stitzinger, he identified four duties of the pastor: 1) teach Holy Scriptures, 2) administer sacraments, 3) participate in the discipline of the church, and 4) care for the needy.

In reviewing the history of Christian ministry, Stitzinger sees two types of reformation and their impact on the ministry: Luther's "Magisterial Reformation" and the "Radical Reformation" associated with the Free-Church thinking of the Anabaptists. "In seeking to understand the contribution of the Reformation to biblical ministry," says Stitzinger, "one must look to both the magisterial reformers (Luther, Bucer, Calvin and Knox) and the Free-Church (true Anabaptists). The former worked under the banner of *reformatio* (reformation), while the latter had *restitutio* (restitution) as its banner."[39]

Stitzinger quotes Michael Sattler to show the Anabaptist's view of the pastoral ministry: "This office [of Pastor] shall be to read, to admonish and teach, to warn, to discipline, to ban in the church, to lead out in prayer for the advancement of all the brethren and sisters, to lift up the bread when it is broken, *and in all things to see to the care of the body of Christ*, in order that it may be built up and developed, and the mouth of the slanderer be stopped"[40] [emphasis supplied]. Pastoral care was given a very high priority in the free church tradition.

Post-Reformation Period

In the post-Reformation church, pastoral care continued to be seen as an important part of the ministry of the church. Puritan pastors, for instance, were to be preachers and caregivers. They

---

38 Stitzinger, 53.
39 Ibid., 51-52.
40 Ibid., 56.

were expected to live a godly life and deliver the message of reconciliation to man. Puritans saw the minister as a "double interpreter," interpreting God to man on the one hand, and interpreting man to God on the other.

Winthrop S. Hudson, in describing the state of the ministry during the Puritan era, talks about the importance given to pastoral care. While preaching was considered the most important pastoral act, pastoral care was considered essential as well. These caregiving duties of the ministers were well defined: "These were the major facets of the minister's pastoral duties—catechizing, visiting, disciplining, and counseling the members of his flock."[41] Visitation was seen as a very important pastoral duty. People were to be prepared for a "fruitful life or a happy death." The pastoral visit was "regarded as a doubly important adjunct because the proper ordering of family life was a major disciplinary concern."[42]

Pastoral counseling was of great concern to the Puritan pastor. According to Hudson, "pastoral counseling was everywhere regarded as one of the most important as well as the most difficult of the pastoral duties."[43] Clergy were highly encouraged to qualify themselves to be good counselors because it was well recognized that unskilled counselors could aggravate the "griefs and perplexities." Many manuals were produced to help pastors deal with difficult cases. A great number of cases dealt with moral perplexities in relation to family life, economic activities, political issues and employment-related problems.

Jonathan Edwards (1703-1758) and other famous pastors of the 18th Century saw themselves as people charged with the care of the saints' souls. Ministry involved honoring God and saving men. Saving men involved serving them in the name of Christ.

John Wesley (1703-1791) was concerned about the spiritual growth and nurture of individuals. He is associated with the

---

41   H. Richard Niebuhr and Daniel D. Williams, eds., *The Ministry in Historical Perspectives* (San Francisco: Harper and Row, 1983), 199.
42   Ibid., 194.
43   Ibid., 196.

doctrine of Christian perfection. William Salsbery states that the ministry of pastoral care experienced a renewal under Wesley's ministry because it was "structured within a biblical framework."[44] In this framework, he found a rationale for developing lay shepherds. Wesley's concept of a lay preacher/pastor was that he was "called, gifted, trained and sent."[45] The lay leaders cared for their classes. The leader was under the supervision of Wesley. Each lay pastor was expected to fulfill the following duties: see each person in the class once a week, meet with the minister and the stewards of the society once a week. The lay preachers provided pastoral shepherding care to such a degree that it was said that "not since the apostolic age had one event exercised so much immediate pastoral care as Wesley did."[46]

The 19th Century provided a good number of faithful shepherds. Charles Spurgeon (1834-1892), widely known for his preaching, was a pastor who saw ministry as meeting the spiritual care needs of people. Stitzinger lists other pastors as examples of good shepherds, such as Charles Bridges (1794-1869) and G. Campbell Morgan (1863-1945).

A Thematic History

Jaekle and Clebsch offer the best thematic history of pastoral care.[47] They found that each historical period was dominated by certain theological themes relating to pastoral care. *Sustaining* was the theme of the early church's pastoral care. The apostles shared the Word. The deacons served the tables. During this period the practitioners of ministry were acknowledged as gifted people.

---

44   William D. Salsbery, "Equipping and Mobilizing Believers to Perform a Shared Ministry of Pastoral Care" (D.Min. Dissertation, Oral Roberts University, 1991), 44.
45   Ibid.
46   Ibid., 43.
47   W.A. Clebsch and C.R. Jaekle, eds., *Pastoral Care in Historical Perspective* (Englewood Cliffs: Prentice-Hall, 1964).

Reconciliation was the theme of the post-Apostolic era (18-306). Pastoral care involved reconciling troubled persons to God. The functional role of the pastor emerged during this period. Ministers began to be paid for their services. By the end of the 3rd Century, buildings were set apart for worship. Major sins and corresponding penalties were identified.

Guiding was the theme of the 4th Century church, according to Jaekle and Clebsch. Pastoral care involved helping people live in accordance with a well-defined Christian culture. The pastoral caregiver was to guide people out of secularism and non-Christian activities into Christian activities.

Guiding continued to be the theme of pastoral care during the "Dark Ages" (500-1400). As monasticism increased, the monks became interpreters of life. Seven deadly sins were identified. A twelve-step ladder of humility was defined.

Healing was the theme of pastoral care for Medieval Christianity (1400-1550). A sacramental system was developed to address the maladies of life. The goal was to restore spiritual and physical health. There was much concern about the activities of demons. Caregivers wanted to provide power for living the Christian life. A sophisticated sacramental system of symbols also developed.

Reconciliation once again became the theme of pastoral care in the post-Reformation (1550-1700) period. Individuals needed reconciliation with God, and internal and external disciplines to live righteous lives. The pastor was able to offer confessional forgiveness. Ministry was seen as requiring special training.

During the Enlightenment (1700-1850), the pastoral theme changed back to *sustaining*. The focus of care was the preservation of faith. John Bunyon wrote *Pilgrim's Progress* during this period.

Evangelism and discipleship became the important issues of the Missionary Era (1850-1907), and *guiding* and *healing* were its pastoral care themes. Establishment of hospitals, YMCA's, and the Salvation Army were expressions of this emphasis.

Reconciliation and *sustaining* were the predominant themes during the Revival period (1908-1919). The first World War caused the need to sustain people.

The next period (1920-1945), which witnessed the Japanese occupation and World War II, required the themes of *healing* and *sustaining,* because the emphasis of ministry became eschatological. The church itself needed preservation and sustaining. Nationalism was incorporated into the ministry.

Jaekle and Clebsch consider the period between 1945 and 1953 the dark age of the modern church. This period witnessed the Korean war; its theme of care was *sustaining.* The following period was a time of rebuilding the church, with the theme of *guiding.* The themes for the sixties were *sustaining* and *guiding.* The seventies was a period of mass evangelism and the pastoral theme was *reconciling.* Jaekle and Clebsch have not extended their evaluation into the 1980s and 1990s; however, one can make a case for the themes of *reconciliation* and *healing.*

In the format used by Jaekle and Clebsch, *healing* directly involved pastoral care. *Sustaining* included Christian education and preservation of traditions. *Guiding* involved devotional life, spiritual direction, leadership training and discipleship. *Reconciliation* dealt with evangelism and the issues of social structure.

Pastoral Care in America

Focusing more clearly on the history of pastoral ministry in America, Sidney Mead says that the concept of ministry among the American Evangelicals underwent considerable change during the first part of the history of Protestantism (1607-1850) in America. Perhaps the greatest change was the loss of the priestly function of ministry. "It is obvious that within this broad context the conception of the minister practically lost its priestly dimension as traditionally conceived, and became that of a consecrated functionary, called of God, who directed the purposive activities of the visible church."[48] The conversion of souls became the primary work of ministers. As a result, the work of a minister was primarily judged by his success in this area. A pastor's care-giving and nurturing skills became secondary. According to Mead, "when pietistic sentiments and revivalist techniques swept to the crest of evangelicalism in America, the conversion of souls tended to crowd out other aspects of ministers' work."[49] This naturally affected the practice of pastoral care.

The important work of E. Brooks Holifield is a noteworthy summary of the history of pastoral care in America through the 1960s. He sees this history as an issue of understanding, as this understanding moves from salvation of the self to "actualization" of the self. "The story proceeds from an ideal of self-denial to one of self-love, from self-love to self-culture, from self-culture to self-mastery, from self-mastery to self-realization within a trustworthy culture, and finally to a later form of self-realization counterposed against cultural mores and social institutions."[50]

The second half of the 19th Century turned out to be a richer time for pastoral care in America. Faced with industrialization, urbanization, and the challenge of Darwinism, the church had to pay special attention to the spiritual needs of people. Although the preaching of the Word still took priority, Christian education and pastoral care also received considerable attention during this period (1850-1950). According to Robert Michaelsen, "Protes-tant ministers have carried on a quietly effective work over the years as pastors, as comforters of the sick, the distressed and the bereaved, as counselors of the perplexed, as guides and guardi-ans to those seeking spiritual light and moral rectitude. But we have seen in the last half century [1900-1950] an increasing awareness of the importance of the minister as pastor."[51] During

---

48 Niebuhr and Williams, 228.
49 Sydney E. Mead, "The Rise of the Evangelical Conception of the Ministry in America: 1607-1850," in Niebuhr and Williams, 244.
50 E. Brooks Holifield, *A History of Pastoral Care in America* (Nashville: Abingdon, 1983), 12.
51 Robert S. Michaelsen, "Protestant Ministry in America: 1850-1950," in Niebuhr and Williams, 250.

this period systematic training in pastoral care became a very important part of the curriculum of seminaries. The clinical training movement was born as a reaction to traditional theological training that did not prepare ministers to deal with the varied personalities of people.

Clinical Pastoral Education (CPE) traces its history to the turbulent twenties, specifically to 1923.[52] Anton Boisen is often called the father of this movement, although Edward E. Thornton, historian of the movement, does not credit the origin of the movement to one man, but instead names three: Richard Cabot, M.D., William S. Keller, M.D., and the Reverend Anton Boisen.[53]

The Association of Professional Chaplains (formerly the College of Chaplains) was founded in 1946 as the Association of Protestant Hospital Chaplains, part of the American Protestant Hospital Association (APHA). Its pioneers included its founding president, Russell L. Dicks, John M. Billinsky, Granger E. Westburg, and John R. Thomas.[54]

Several other pastoral care organizations developed in the United States in the 20th Century. They include the Association of Mental Health Clergy (AMHC), the American Association of Pastoral Counselors (AAPC), the American Protestant Correctional Chaplains Association (APCCA), the National Association of Catholic Chaplains (NACC), the National Association of Jewish Chaplains (NAJC), and the National Association of Business and Industrial Chaplains (NIBIC). The history of pastoral care associations includes the story of improvement in pastoral training in caregiving skills, development of standards for certification, and, naturally, some rivalries, collaborations and mergers.

---

52   Edward E. Thornton, *Professional Education for Ministry* (Nashville: Abingdon, 1970).
53   Ibid., 41.
54   *Caregiver Journal* 2, no. 1, 6-9.

Modern Spirit-Led Pastoral Care

Clinical Pastoral Education was a reactionary movement, too liberal even for the liberals. The conservative Pentecostals were not involved in the initial history of this movement. The Pentecostal movement, which began around 1900, was focused on the saving of souls, and not on caring for souls. The classical Pentecostals in the beginning, and the charismatics and "Third-Wavers" after them, kept the same emphasis. While divine healing was a theological characteristic of the Pentecostals, the denominational and independent charismatics emphasized healing as a major ministry theme. Although healing was a pastoral concern among all "Full Gospel" believers, the method of ministry used was often evangelistic. In this sense pastoral care did not receive widespread attention among Pentecostals and charismatics.

In the second half of this century, Pentecostal pastors were influenced by developments in other helping professions. Many pastors attempted to improve their counseling skills by attending clergy training offered by community mental health centers and other agencies during the 1960s and 1970s. No systematic account of this influence is available, although individual testimonies exist. Pastors were also influenced by Christian psychological writers such as Clyde Narramore and Jay Adams.

A few Pentecostal ministers began to develop their skills and write on the subject of pastoral care and counseling. Prominent among them are Richard Dobbins, Raymond Brock, and Robert Crick.

An Assemblies of God assistant district superintendent as well as psychologist and writer, Richard Dobbins has had a tremendous influence on the Assemblies of God. His *Emerge Ministries* counseling center in Akron, Ohio, specializes in counseling ministers and in offering counselor training to ministers.

As a prolific writer, educator, and veteran missionary, Raymond Brock enjoyed considerable influence in Pentecostal circles.

Robert Crick, as the first bona fide Pentecostal to be fully certified as a CPE supervisor, has had a great impact on Pentecostals in general and the Church of God denomination in particular.

In the 1970s and 1980s some charismatic CPE supervisors and others emerged who were sympathetic to charismatics and Pentecostals. Robert Yarrington of the state hospital in Connecticut was known as a charismatic CPE supervisor in New England; Ken Blank of Oklahoma became known as a supervisor sympathetic to charismatics.

Pentecostal ministers and seminarians began to enter CPE training in the late 1960s and early 1970s. This author experienced a year-long CPE residency at Norwich State Hospital in Norwich, Connecticut in June 1975.

The Assemblies of God have been supportive of CPE training of chaplain candidates, with some reservations. This denomination affirmed the ministry of pastoral care by establishing the Commission on Chaplains to endorse chaplains for various ministries, primarily military chaplaincy. This support has grown through the years. Today the Commission endorses chaplains for multiple ministries.

Other Pentecostal denominations have similar endorsing bodies. The independent charismatics have an endorsing agency known as the Chaplaincy for Full Gospel Churches. The activities of these organizations have been growing steadily. In fact, a 1996 guest editorial in the *Journal of Pastoral Care* was written by David B. Plummer, director of the Chaplaincy for Full Gospel Churches organization founded by Chaplain Col. Jim Ammerman (Ret.). Plummer now leads the endorsing agency Coalition of Spirit-filled Churches.

The discomfort of the Pentecostals concerning CPE training was based on the often painful experience of Pentecostals who entered CPE training. For most Pentecostal trainees, CPE was a wilderness experience. This author, like many other Pentecostals,

CPE   Clinical Pastoral education

can relate to John K. Vining's experience;[55] however, in many ways this author had a more positive experience. Each individual experience depends much on the supervisor involved. Overall, the outcome of CPE has been very satisfactory.

Three special issues kept the early Pentecostals from developing the area of pastoral care. First was the charismatic aspect of their worship. Ministry often took place in church; since the Holy Spirit was doing the ministry, the pastor's skills were not a matter of great concern.

The second issue was the puritanical holiness to which most Pentecostals were committed. This meant that many issues that needed pastoral care were seen as disciplinary issues. Concern for the pain of the divorced person, for example, was less important than the concern to discipline the divorced to prevent more divorces from occurring. For Pentecostals, pastoral care was not the main issue in such cases.

Third, Pentecostals were committed to eschatological evangelism. This position encouraged evangelism at all cost on all occasions. Thus, a funeral was not a place to minister to the grieving and bereaved as much as it was an opportunity to win the lost souls who would be attending the service. Since Jesus might come any day, no one should leave unsaved.

There were many Pentecostal pastors who gave a high level of pastoral care to their people, but this was not the norm. Most pastors were untrained in the area of pastoral care, as Bible colleges and institutes did not offer much in this area. Gifted caregivers and self-directed learners did much better than others.

Pastoral care among charismatics depended on the kind of charismatics involved. Mainline charismatics generally had trained pastors; independent charismatics generally preferred the evangelistic healing approach. Megachurches among charismatics were focused on the sanctuary, and not geared toward Chris-

---

55   John K. Vining and Edward E. Decker, eds., *Soul Care: A Pentecostal/Charismatic Perspective* (East Rockaway, NY: Cummings and Hathaway Publishers, 1996), 121-128.

tian education or pastoral care. This focus is changing in positive ways.

Ironically, the person God used more than anyone else to promote pastoral care as a valuable part of the healing process was a healing evangelist. When Oral Roberts built the massive City of Faith complex in Tulsa, Oklahoma, it included a hospital, clinics, and a medical research center. "Healing teams" were formed, composed of physicians, pastoral caregivers, nurses and other medical personnel. These pioneering teams were to bring healing to sick people by "merging medicine and prayer." This merging of medicine and prayer was the founding principle of the City of Faith hospital. At one time there were nearly forty staff prayer partners (chaplains and pastoral counselors) under the leadership of Col. Duie Jernigan, a retired military chaplain who headed the Spiritual Care Division of the organization. Col. Jernigan was both an ordained minister and a licensed psychologist, and most staff members were clinically trained. Oral Roberts Ministries invested millions of dollars in this vision of providing spiritual care for patients alongside excellent medical care.

The City of Faith experiment, while not a financial success, impacted the entire medical world. Spiritual care of patients in hospitals and use of clergy on interdisciplinary teams soon became an acceptable idea to many people who previously had reservations about ministers being involved in hospital treatment teams. At the same time, medical treatment became a newly acceptable option to many people of Pentecostal faith. In recognition of his contribution to the world of medicine and pastoral care, the College of Chaplains honored Oral Roberts by inviting him to be the keynote speaker at their 1983 annual convention held in San Diego. It was my privilege to attend that convention, where I was received as a fellow of the College of Chaplains.

Hundreds of volunteers were trained as lay caregivers at the City of Faith. Students from the Oral Roberts University School of Theology were trained in chaplaincy, first through field education courses, and eventually through CPE when City of Faith was accredited as a CPE center offering basic and advanced training. Herbert Hillebrand, former president of the College of

Chaplains, and Ken Blank, CPE Supervisor at Presbyterian Hospital in Oklahoma City, were the CPE supervisors at City of Faith. Many charismatics and Pentecostals received pastoral care training and experience at this first Spirit-led CPE center.

Spirit-led theological seminaries have done much to enhance the quality of pastoral care in Full Gospel churches. The Assemblies of God Theological Seminary offered courses in pastoral care and clinical ministry from its very beginning. The Church of God Theological Seminary also has maintained a strong pastoral care and counseling program. Oral Roberts University School of Theology not only has a strong pastoral care program, but it also has several degree programs in Christian counseling. The impact of these institutions on the ministry of pastoral care in Full Gospel churches has been significant.

Pentecostal and charismatic periodicals in recent years have given much space to the subject of pastoral care and counseling. Denominational magazines, such as *Pentecostal Evangel* and *Enrichment,* and charismatic periodicals, such as *Ministries Today* and *Charisma,* have made an effort to include articles relevant to pastoral caregivers in the local churches.

Pastoral caregivers have always maintained informal networks of persons for their own support and encouragement. These networks normally begin at denominational gatherings and meetings of professional organizations. It was only natural that eventually a formal network of caregivers would be born. The first such meeting took place in Atlanta in 1995. John Vining of the Church of God Theological Seminary and Edward Decker of Oral Roberts University School of Theology were instrumental in organizing this first conference of Spirit-led caregivers and counselors. The response of participants was encouraging, and the outcome so satisfactory that a decision was made for an annual event.

The second conference of Spirit-led caregivers and counselors was held in January, 1996, at Oral Roberts University. Hundreds of caregivers and counselors attended this meeting. Keynote addresses were given by Francis MacNutt, Richard Dobbins,

Edward Decker, John Vining, Steven Land and Thomson Mathew. Focus groups met to discuss various topics of common interest and stimulating ideas were discussed at several workshops. Among topics discussed were the possibility of a doctoral program in counseling through a consortium of Full Gospel schools, and plans for publication of materials.

It was not surprising that a resolution proposing the formation of the Fellowship of Pentecostal/Charismatic Caregivers (FPCC) was passed at the business meeting held at that conference: "Be it resolved that we in humility and servanthood form a continuing fellowship that follows the work of the Holy Spirit and affirms the callings of ministry that have been placed upon each of us." The FPCC was formally organized a year later.

The formation of the Fellowship of Pentecostal/Charismatic Caregivers is a significant event in the evolving story of Pentecostal pastoral care. It has the potential of impacting the Full Gospel churches in the way the formation of CPE impacted mainline denominations. Discussions are already under way to consider the formation of a Pentecostal form of clinical training. Only time will tell how much of this potential will be realized.

A Look Ahead

These are exciting days for individuals involved in the care of souls among Full Gospel people. One can feel a sense of destiny in being a part of this group of people. With that awareness upon me, I wish to conclude this historical account by making the following statements for consideration by Spirit-led caregivers.

First, we must discern the times and speak prophetically to our own constituency concerning the need to intentionally promote pastoral care and pastoral healing alongside evangelistic forms of healing.

Second, it is time to speak prophetically to our counterparts in mainline denominations. We must ask our colleagues to consider what the Spirit is doing in the world today. They must be challenged to look to what God is doing in our midst. We are half a billion believers who are neither theologically deficient nor insignificant. We must not hide our light under a bushel. We must encourage our denominational colleagues to seek biblical spiritual gifts rather than the false promises of New Age spirituality.

Third, we must continue to practice Spirit-led caregiving with maximum integrity; we must never try to hide any personal incompetence under the cover of so-called gifts. We must prepare ourselves through proper training to do skillful caregiving, and then surrender those skills to the Master. Let our skills become in God's hands the five loaves that would feed five thousand and more. Let us open ourselves to God and allow his Holy Spirit to flow though us, empowering others to experience true wholeness in the name of Jesus Christ our Lord.

Note: The best way for caregivers to access the writings of the church fathers is to use Thomas C. Oden's four-volume collection, *Classical Pastoral Care* (1987-94), published by Baker Books. Due to the format requirements of this volume, details on the original sources are not given here. Oden supplies full references.

2

A Pentecostal Theology
of Pastoral Ministry

Background

Pastoral care in Pentecostal and charismatic churches is presently in need of a solid theological foundation. Neither individuals in need of care nor the Pentecostal/charismatic Spirit-led movement will receive greatest benefit from each pastor practicing his own version of pastoral care. There must be sound theology supporting effective pastoral care.

The serious neglect of pastoral care evident in some Spirit-led churches indicates a prevailing lack of theological depth. We must never forget that church growth accomplished at the expense of pastoral care cannot be maintained.

On the other hand, pastoral care in the mainline denominations has been under the potential threat of being swallowed up by unscrutinized psychology. Some have forgotten that pastoral care has been a theological discipline for two thousand years. Shepherding is a biblical concept, able to stand on its own and speak its own language. Pastoral care as a biblical ministry must retain

Dr. Matthew offers a philosophy of Pastoral Care [handwritten]

its biblical and historical identity. Even a high-tech society
stands in need of old fashioned high-touch shepherding. In the
tug of war between pro-psychology and anti-psychology wings
of Christians, pastoral care should be allowed to establish its
own clear theological identity.

A Personal Theology

There is no ideal Pentecostal theology of pastoral care to point
to; however, there are biblical principles which can be used in
developing one's personal version of pastoral care theology for
Pentecostal pastors. In my attempt to merge my theological and
clinical education with my Pentecostal heritage and pastoral
experience, I have compiled a personal theology that I would
like to present as my contribution toward the development of a
truly comprehensive Pentecostal theology of pastoral care.

Webster defines *ministry* as "the office, duties, or functions of
a minister." Obviously, much is missing from this definition.
Ministry is a holistic response to God's call; in this sense ministry is both personal and vocational.

Christian ministry is deeply rooted in Judaism. These roots,
according to James Wharton, show ministry as not only individual acts of compassion and comfort, but a special quality of
relationship between God and people, and between priests and
people. Ministry is modeled after God's relationship with Israel.
"Ministry to human others is, in the ultimate sense, ministry to
God."[56] The Hebrew word *abodah* (service) really means "worship" when it is offered to God. God wants us to offer this service for our own sakes, not his.[57]

Wharton sees every human interaction as an occasion for ministry. "In every human contact the ministry of God to Israel, and
Israel to God, will either be expressed or fail to be expressed to

---

56   James Wharton, cited in Earl E. Shelp and Ronald Sunderland, eds., *A
     Biblical Basis for Ministry* (Philadelphia: Westminster, 1981), 20.
57   Shelp and Sunderland, 37.

some degree."[58] We therefore accept the fact that our service will always be imperfect until the time of perfection comes. It is essential to serve in humility, since God has used some very unlikely candidates in ministry. A biblical ministry must also involve freedom, celebration, and a sense of humor.

Samuel Karff, a Jewish scholar, defines ministry somewhat differently. To him, ministry represents the caring response of the community of faith to the universal experience of human suffering. Ministry offers a tangible opportunity to express compassionate concern for another. "It opens one to the pain of the world.... It offers each the possibility of encountering the shechina, as one who dwells with his people."[59]

Paul J. Achtemeir believes that the Gospels were vehicles of ministry for each writer and resources for ministry within the primitive Christian communities. Ministry is doing "what we can, in word and deed, to spread the good news among people so that they, realizing the redemption that awaits them, may share the joyful anticipation of God's final, glorious, rule."[60] Thus our resource for pastoral ministry is the confidence that ultimately God cannot be defeated.

The story of Jesus washing the disciples' feet is a statement of the Johannine understanding of ministry. John illustrates that ministry is grounded in the belief that God is love and that he reveals himself in love. John sees conversion of people as vital to ministry. It is love that converts, for God so loved the world that the world must be converted. Ministers are friends of Jesus in this work of the ministry; ministry, then, is friendship with Jesus.

Having been raised in a Hindu nation, I find my impressions of ministry tremendously influenced by Paul, the apostle to the Gentiles. Paul's ministry was grounded in his theology, and his theology in turn was shaped by the context of his ministry. Paul ministered as a preacher, apostle and teacher. His ministry was

---

58   Ibid., 61.
59   Samuel Karff, cited in Shelp and Sunderland, 100.
60   Paul J. Achtemeir, cited in Shelp and Sunderland, 185.

both pastoral and prophetic. Paul was a facilitator. As Victor Furnish points out, a facilitator is more than just a convenor, discussion starter, resource person, or business manager.[61]

Paul's writings to the Corinthian church vividly demonstrate his understanding of the theology of pastoral care ministry. Furnish points out four characteristics of Paul: (1) he had a pastoral commitment to the Corinthians, (2) he made deeply perceptive theological analyses of their situations, (3) he kept a determined reiteration of the "theology of the cross," and (4) he never lost his keen sense of call.[62]

Important Questions Arise

How shall we define ministry in the 21st Century? Is ministry just one of the helping professions? If Jesus and Paul are the models for authentic ministry, how does their kind of ministry become practical in today's world?

Henri J.M. Nouwen struggled with such questions in his classic work, *The Wounded Healer*, offering us a modern definition of ministry. Nouwen believes that modern man is, above all, a suffering man. Psychologically wounded due to lack of hope and loneliness, man faces the predicament of rootlessness. Nuclear man normally tries to break out of this predicament through one of two routes: the *mystical way*, or the *revolutionary way*. Nouwen believes that man needs a third alternative, which he calls the *Christian way*. Here the mystical and revolutionary come together in Jesus to help the modern man find liberation.

The minister must go beyond his professional role and be a fellow human being with his own wounds and suffering. In other words, modern ministers must become willing to be wounded healers. A wounded healer should not be bleeding himself. He

---

61   Shelp and Sunderland, 136.
62   Ibid., 137-142.

must be a person of prayer, a person who "has to pray, and who has to pray always."[63]

According to Nouwen, a Christian minister must have:

- Personal concern for others,

- Faith in the value and meaning of life, and

- Hope.

"The beginning and the end of all Christian leadership is to give your life for others."[64]

One cannot be led out of the desert by another who has never traveled that route. The real motivation for leading others into the future in the *Christian way* is **hope**. "Hope makes it possible to look beyond the fulfillment of urgent wishes ... and offers a vision beyond human suffering and even death."[65]

Paul taught that God's strength is made perfect in our weaknesses (2 Cor 12:9). Nouwen teaches that the minister must be aware of his own weaknesses and pain. This will enable one to "convert his weakness into strength and to offer his own experience as a source of healing."[66] The exciting part about Nouwen's proposal is that he believes that personal spirituality is extremely important for all who minister. "While a doctor can still be a good doctor even when his private life is severely disrupted, no minister can offer service without a constant and vital acknowledgment of his own experiences."[67]

Unlike the physician, the minister's primary task is not to take away pain. According to Nouwen, the minister's main task is to prevent people from suffering for the wrong reasons. The Christian minister accomplishes this through his hospitality.

---

63 Henri J.M. Nouwen, *The Wounded Healer* (Garden City: Doubleday, 1972), 47.
64 Ibid., 72.
65 Ibid., 76.
66 Ibid., 89.
67 Ibid., 90.

Hospitality is the virtue which allows us to break through the nervousness of our own fears and to open our spiritual houses to the stranger, with the intuition that salvation comes to us in the form of a tired traveler.[68]

In his work *Creative Ministry,* Nouwen examines the question of pastoral responsibilities and lists the primary responsibilities of the minister as:

- Teaching,

- Preaching,

- Counseling,

- Organizing, and

- Celebrating.[69]

The ministry is carried out by fulfilling these tasks. However, the ministerial functions are vitally connected to the minister's own spiritual life. Through teaching, preaching, counseling, organizing and celebrating, the minister is actually laying down his life for his friends. This is what makes ministry unique.

Seward Hiltner divides pastoral responsibilities somewhat differently in his *Preface to Pastoral Theology.* Hiltner lists them as:

- Healing,

- Sustaining,

- Guiding,

- Communicating, and

- Organizing.[70]

---

68 Ibid., 91.
69 Henri J.M. Nouwen, *Creative Ministry* (Garden City: Image, 1971), 110.
70 Seward Hiltner, *Preface to Pastoral Counseling* (Nashville: Abingdon, 1958), 89-171.

W.A. Clebsch and C.R. Jaekle divide pastoral responsibilities into four areas:

- Healing,
- Sustaining,
- Guiding, and
- Reconciling.[71]

Pastoral Authority

Samuel Southard lists, in his *Pastoral Authority in Personal Relationships,* four sources of authority over Christians:

- Authority t hat c omes f rom o bedience to t he w ill o f God (Acts 5:29, 1 Thes 4:1);

- Authority d erived from t he L ordship of C hrist (Mt 7:28, 29; Jn 13:13);

- Authority of the church and its leaders; and

- Authority of those who exercise lawful authority in the world.[72]

A minister's authority comes first from the *call.* H. Richard Niebuhr lists four distinct calls in the life of a minister:

- The call to be a Christian,
- The secret call,
- The providential call, and
- The ecclesiastical call.[73]

---

71 Clebsch and Jaekle, 8-10.
72 Samuel Southard, *Pastoral Authority in Personal Relationships* (Nashville: Abingdon, 1969), 20.
73 H. R ichard N iebuhr, *The P urpose o f t he C hurch a nd I ts M inistry* (New York: Harper and Brothers, 1956), 64.

There is a process of authentication that confirms the authority of the minister. However, "the real personal authority arises out of the concrete incarnation of the spirit of loving service which by God's help becomes present in the care of souls."[74]

Jesus is the model of authority for a minister (Mt 9:8, 22:18). Jesus made it clear that he had authority (Lk 4:32), and that his authority came from God (Jn 8:28). He believed this kind of authority did not conform to the model of authority of the world (Mt 20:25-28). This authority made him a servant, not a master. Note that Jesus himself imposed great limitations upon his own power (Mt 4, 20:20-28; Lk 12:13, 14) and he delegated authority to his disciples (Mt 10:1, 28:18; Mk 6:7).

Southard believes that pastoral authority involves at least three themes:

- Discipleship,

- Craftsmanship, and

- Reconciliation.

Southard reminds us that pastoral authority is not conferred on account of personal superiority; the minister is a person among persons, set apart for the work of reconciliation. In this work of reconciliation, the authority of the minister can be manifested in different forms, such as prophetic, evangelistic, pastoral, priestly, and organizational authority.[75] "The authority of the minister is basically his ability to bring a transcendent power to bear upon our lives."[76] "The minister is accepted as an authority when he demonstrates godly character and communicates the presence of a power beyond himself."[77] This kind of authority is applicable regardless of the location of ministry. This is good news for ministers who are engaged in ministries outside the local church.

---

74 Daniel D. Williams, *The Ministry and the Care of Souls* (New York: Harper and Row, 1961), 43.
75 Southard, *Pastoral Authority,* 16.
76 Ibid.
77 Ibid., 61.

Purpose of Ministry

What are the message and mission of ministry? The message of ministry is still the message of the good news of the Kingdom of God. The mission is to make disciples by going, teaching, and healing (Mt 28:18, Mk 3:14, 15). How are these disciples made? The Church is called a temple, a place of worship and fellowship (1 Cor 3:16). The Church is also described as a building made with living stones, each one cemented in place by the mortar of love (1 Pet 2:5, 1 Cor 13).

Of all the biblical images of the Church, Paul's concept of the Church as a body with many members appeals most to me. The Bible says that the Church is a body with many members who have various functions (1 Cor 12). A body is not an organization, but an organism. A body has many parts, and each part has a vital function. In the Church, the function of each member can be called ministry.

As a person is greater than the sum of his body parts, so is the Church greater than the sum of its members. As it fulfills God's purposes in the world, the Church's ministry is greater than the sum of the ministries of its members.

God has placed the Church in the world for his own purposes. History reveals that the Church has understood these purposes differently at different times. Its understanding of these purposes evolves and is influenced by changes in culture.

George W. Weber talks about the "rethinking" of the purposes of the modern church.[78] He says the Church is changing its purpose from "taking Christ to the world" to "joining him." Weber suggests that the Church is changing its goal from proselytism to mission. The emphasis is no longer on "winning," but on "witnessing."

---

78 George W. Weber, *Today's Church: A Community of Exiles and Pilgrims* (Nashville: Abingdon, 1979), 27-31.

My own experience on both sides of the missions effort, as a missionary and as a member of a target group, leads me to see this change as significant. This new thinking about outreach is more in line with the biblical purposes of the Church, which was formed in this world to *witness* to the world.

Winning is a concept well suited to American culture, but the term "witnessing" reflects a biblical approach. We do not have to "win the world for God" because it is already his. We do need to witness to the world about the undying love of the patiently waiting Heavenly Father. An ordained minister is set apart for a life of bearing witness.

A witness is one who can share something he or she has heard, seen, or experienced. A witness is one who can testify, "I was blind, but now I see." This ministry of witnessing carries a responsibility to testify of experience, but not to make the decision for the lost one. A witness should not feel a need to force anyone into the kingdom. A wise witness realizes that those who are coerced or frightened into the kingdom seldom remain in it.

In J.C. Hoekendijk's book *The Church Inside Out*, the goal of the Church is defined as e vangelism. He argues that the word "evangelize" has come to represent a biblical camouflage of what should rightly be called "the reconquest of ecclesiastical influence."[79] Hoekendijk explains that the true aim of evangelism is to establish the *shalom*. And *shalom* is much more than personal salvation. It is at once peace, integrity, community, harmony and justice.[80]

According to Hoekendijk, *shalom* is to be proclaimed (*kerygma*), lived (*koinonia*), and demonstrated in humble service (*diakonia*). If the goal of the Church is to establish *shalom*, then ministry is being involved in these three aspects of evangelism.

---

79   J.C. Hoekendijk, *The Church Inside Out* (Philadelphia: Westminster, 1966), 15.
80   Ibid., 21.

Recent Writings

Henri Nouwen's later writings dealt with these aspects of ministry. Particularly, he saw ministry as service in the name of Jesus. His moving reflections on ministry as humble leadership in service of others challenges this generation which seems to have accepted arrogance—in various pretenses—as a needed virtue of leaders.[81]

Recent writers have struggled in other ways with the images of ministry in the 20th Century. Donald Messer points out several contemporary stereotypes of ministers as hired hands, sexless servants, and superhuman saints. Messer offers a definition of ministers as:

- Wounded healers in a community of the compassionate,

- Servant leaders in a servant church,

- Political mystics in a prophetic community,

- Enslaved liberators of a rainbow church, and

- Practical theologians in a post-denominational church.[82]

Among recent writers, probably the best historical review of the Christian ministry from a Protestant perspective is Thomas Oden's notable work, *Pastoral Theology: Essentials of Ministry*.[83] Oden reminds us of the importance of the call and the shepherding aspects of ministry. John MacArthur, Jr., in his collection, *Rediscovering Pastoral Ministry,* calls contemporary ministers back to the biblical mandates of ministry.

---

81 Henri J.M. Nouwen, *In the Name of Jesus* (New York: Crossroad, 1989).

82 Donald E. Messer, *Contemporary Images of Christian Ministry* (Nashville: Abingdon, 1989).

83 Thomas C. Oden, *Pastoral Theology: Essentials of Ministry* (San Francisco: Harper and Row, 1983).

Holy Spirit in Ministry

Pastoral ministry is deeply rooted in its biblical heritage. History has molded and shaped ministry to prepare it to face changing, challenging needs.

Unfortunately, what seems to be missing in most Western writings describing ministry is any significant attention to the work of the Holy Spirit in ministry. This is a glaring deficiency, because ministry cannot be a totally human enterprise. Human understanding and skills are insufficient for the accomplishment of God's ministry. Ministry can be made effective only by the enabling, empowering presence and work of the Holy Spirit.

Contemporary images of ministry suffer from an imbalance between love and power, appearing as love without power, or power without love, instead of the ideal ministry of Holy Spirit-empowered love.

Jesus claimed that the Spirit of the Lord was upon him and acted in that power. He instructed his disciples to tarry in Jerusalem until they would receive the Holy Spirit, which would come upon them in power. We know they did not expand their ministries until after the day of Pentecost. This is because there is no successful ministry without the presence and guidance of the Holy Spirit, the One who enables. As the Paraclete, the Holy Spirit dwells within us to enable and empower our work in the ministry. We must allow the Spirit to move in and through our lives.

An ordained minister is set apart to bear witness, and this witness must be Spirit-enabled to be powerful. The ordained minister is the set-apart representative of a powerful God, and God's power is intended to be expressed through him or her.

A minister must therefore be open to the operation of the gifts of the Spirit in his or her life. When these gifts are allowed to operate—with discernment, wisdom and humility—people's needs are met and God's name is glorified. However, such a Spirit-empowered ministry is often a short-lived ministry if the minister does not seek to grow in the fruits of the Spirit. The very essence of ministry is the first fruit of the Spirit, a Holy Spirit-empowered love that is unlimited because it is empowered by God (Gal 5:22).

Thus witnessing becomes far more than just sharing a vocal testimony; witnessing becomes a fruitful existence as the light of the world and the salt of the earth. Love is the best tool of evangelism, and loving is the best form of witnessing. The purpose of the church is to let the world taste God's love, and ministry is the way its members offer the world that taste. The best way to be incarnational in ministry, to carry incarnational presence into daily encounters, is to allow the gifts and fruits of the Spirit to manifest in one's life.

The person of the minister is very important in the work of the ministry. A good minister is a wounded healer himself, because personal strengths and weaknesses can all be resources in ministry. Ministry presents many responsibilities, but authority has been granted to the minister to carry out these responsibilities.

As Jesus is our model of ministry, ministry is serving and bearing witness. True witnessing has to do with loving. This love is born of the Spirit and is manifested in the gifts and fruits of the Spirit. Both members and ordained ministers express this love through the empowerment of the Holy Spirit's gifts and the fruit in their lives.

The Ministry of Healing:
Theological Presuppositions

A Spirit-led ministry of healing is based on certain presuppositions.

First is the assumption that health and illness are both dynamic in nature. Health is not merely the absence of illness, but a wholeness of being. Wholeness is that aspect of being human that defies fragmentation in body, mind, and spirit.

A second assumption is that human beings are unitary. In other words, the human body, mind and spirit are "fearfully and wonderfully" interwoven at profoundly deep levels. Each aspect of human life interacts with and influences every other aspect, which means that when one part of a person is hurting, he hurts throughout his body, mind and spirit.

This leads to a third assumption that the individual is able, knowingly or unknowingly, to affect his or her own state of wellness or illness. Personal attitude, habits of discipline, and priorities and choices one makes have much to do with one's wholeness or lack of health. The faith or personal theology of an individual is a potential resource for health or hindrance to wellness. For example, one person's theology may burden him with guilt and condemnation, by attributing his illness to personal sin, negative thinking, or negative confession, while another person's theology sets him free from condemnation. While one person's faith helps the healing process, another's faith helps her face with grace the final human experience of physical death.

A Spirit-led ministry of healing is based on additional theological presuppositions:

- God is a good God, and he wants us to be whole. The New Testament word *soteria*, like the Old Testament word *shalom*, carries with it connotations of salvation, healing, preservation, and harmony in relationships.

- God is the source of *all* healing. Whether the healing results from medical intervention, faith-filled thoughts and
  prayer, natural biological restorative processes, or a com-
  bination of these, all healing comes from God. Growing up
  in a Pentecostal church that did not rely much on medical
  healing, I personally found this teaching of Oral Roberts to
  be revelatory and freeing.

- Divine intervention in the lives of individuals in need is
  always a real possibility. This cannot be guaranteed for
  each person in terms of time and place, but it can certainly
  be expected. A minister can sincerely pray for divine in-
  terventions or miracles. It is safe to assume that God can
  and may intervene at any point to bring about the kind of
  healing that he wants in any particular situation. This is
  why the New Testament commands us to pray for and
  have faith for healings.

- Healing occurs in several modes. Sometimes healing
  comes instantaneously; at other times it comes more
  gradually. Sometimes healing comes as a consequence of
  medical intervention, sometimes as a result of prayer.

- Sometimes people are not healed physically; all die once,
  usually sooner than they would choose. For believers in
  resurrection, this ultimate experience is acceptable because
  Hebrews 9:27 teaches us that it is appointed for us once to
  die. For a Christian, death is not a defeat. Certainly death
  brings grief and sorrow, but we do not sorrow as those
  who have no hope. We sorrow as those who have the hope
  of eternal life. This is a very important concept because, in
  the final analysis, all physical healing is temporary.

- Suffering and death are realities of life in this fallen world.
  Comfort can always be sought in the presence of the Holy
  Spirit.

- Healing is for wholeness, not for perfection. True wholeness, because it involves body, mind and spirit, issues
  from a Christ-centered life of discipleship.

- Wholeness involves all aspects of one's life: physical, spiritual, emotional, relational, economic, and environmental.

- There is such a thing called the fullness of time (*kairos*). Healing occurs in the fullness of time.

- Healing is enhanced by the things that nourish the spirit—such as love (1 Jn 4:7), hope (Psa 42:5, 11), faith (Mt 9:22), the will to live (Jn 5:6), and laughter (Phil 4:4).

- The Body of Christ is entrusted with the ministry of healing. The Body of Christ must guard against inadvertently promoting illness.

- Pastoral counseling is extended altar ministry.

- Christian acceptance heals. The great miracle that changed the life of the Samaritan woman was that Jesus accepted her even though he knew everything she had ever done (Jn 4:29).

- Caring heals. True caring happens when one is willing to give up one's own agenda to consider another's, as Christ gave himself for us (Phil 2:6, 7).

- Persons engaged in the healing ministry of Jesus must consider that they are themselves signs and wonders of God's doing. They themselves are living human documents exhibiting the grace of God.

Pastoral Ministry of Healing

A pastoral healing ministry is an extension of the ministry of Jesus. In a place of paradox, such as a hospital, a minister must represent the presence of Jesus. With the life-giving Spirit of Jesus in him, a minister can be an incarnational presence to hurting people, a "living reminder of Jesus," as Nouwen would say. Motivated by God's love and enabled by his Spirit, a caregiver becomes a channel of God's grace. As one ministers in the name of Christ, this grace impacts other people's lives.

A minister of the Gospel has certain resources at his disposal. Primary among these resources is the minister's own sense of self as a sinner saved by the grace of God. Other powerful resources described by William Hulme are prayer, faith, sacraments, Scripture, counseling skills, and the Christian community.[84]

An effective minister must be able to initiate, maintain and appropriately terminate healthy relationships. It is within the context of these relationships between pastoral shepherd and flock that the most effective ministry can happen. God so loved the world that he sent his Son to heal the broken relationship with the world. One can rely on personal resources and pastoral authority to establish healing relationships. The Holy Spirit is allowed to work in and through these relationships to bring healing and wholeness to persons.

---

84 William Hulme, *Pastoral Care and Counseling*, (Minneapolis: Augsburg, 1981).

3

Caring: The Heart
of Pastoral Care

Definition

Webster defines *caring* as "be(ing) concerned about." I would define caring as "concern expressed." Caring is an attitude of concern that is communicated in some form. Caring is not godly caring until it is *expressed*. I am convinced that there are sincerely caring churches that do not grow because their care is not expressed in an understandable fashion. There are caring couples getting divorced because they have failed in communicating their care to one another. True caring must be expressed. Expressing care, however, requires skills.

Caring is loving, and loving has to do with giving. "God so loved the world that he *gave* ..." (Jn 3:16). Caring is a ministry of giving, but one cannot give that which one does not have. In order to give care, one must receive care. In order to give care regularly, one must have received care. God does not expect us to give from our emptiness: "Freely you have received, freely give." (Mt 10:8). Sometimes our caregiving is poor because our care receiving has been poor. We must receive care from our loving God, caring family, and the members of the body of Christ. Every pastor needs a pastor and a peer group with whom he or she can be transparent. An excellent source of care for a minister is a peer group that cares enough to confront and "provoke us to love and good work."

Caring is accepting; only one that experiences acceptance can offer acceptance. Caring is empathizing; only one who is in touch with his or her own feelings can offer true empathy. Caring is listening; only one that has been listened to can listen well to others. Caring is confronting. Only one who knows the difference between conviction and condemnation can "speak the truth in love." Caring involves attending, responding, loving, and risking rejection. In effect, caring has to do with initiating healthy helping relationships, maintaining such relationships, and in time, appropriately terminating them.

Characteristics of Caregivers

Caregivers must be genuine. One cannot pretend to be caring; humans easily identify a phony when they see one. Caring has to be genuine self-giving, which is costly. God gave much to care for us.

A caregiver needs a balanced self-image. A person with poor self-esteem gives a poor quality of care. Conversely, a person who thinks too highly of himself also gives poor care. Often such a person covers up his or her poor self-esteem with a "holier than thou" façade.

What is pastoral care? Pastoral care is, simply and *uniquely*, care given by a pastor. In larger contexts involving a flock too large for one shepherd, it may be defined as "shepherdly" care. Although there are several groups of professional caregivers, pastoral care is unique because it represents care given by a man or woman of God in the name of Jesus and under the authority of a minister of the Gospel. As such, pastoral care represents heritage, authority, and meaning. Pastoral care is a ministry of maintaining a dialogue with the world while one is in dialogue with God.

It is said that pastoral care arises out of the push of the pastoral calling and the pull of human need.[85] In some people there is a special gift that creates the Christian response to humanity's hurt; in others this response must be cultivated. Caring is a response to human need, but this response is relative to the caregiver's understanding of humanity and relationship with the Holy Spirit.

Caring as Relationship

Some of us have a liberal understanding of humankind; others are more conservative in their views. The Pentecostal pastor has a fundamentalist understanding of man. As a believer of "the inspired and only infallible and authoritative Word of God," his or her understanding is strictly according to the Bible. It includes the story of man's fall and God's plan of redemption.

Scripture speaks of humans in terms of their relationships. The story of Adam is a good illustration of this fact: we see Adam as a wholesome person enjoying three healthy relationships: first, his relationship with God (vertical); second, his relationship with his fellow creatures (horizontal); and third, his relationship with his own self.

It seems that what happened as a result of the fall was a loss in the perfection of these relationships. Following his disobedience, man began to hide himself from God's presence (broken vertical relationship). He began to blame his fellow human being and the snake (broken horizontal relationships). He became ashamed of his very self, and began to look for things to cover his nakedness (broken relationship with self).

It has been man's struggle ever since to reestablish these broken relationships. This has also been God's desire and plan, so

---

85 C.W. Brister, *Pastoral Care in the Church* (New York: Harper and Row, 1964), 7.

he has revealed himself to humankind in and through history.
Man has sought his reconciliation through sacrifices and even
idolatry. Calvary became inevitable, because what happened on
Calvary was God's revelation of himself. Ultimately, in the form
of a man, the man from Nazareth paid the price of full reconciliation.

Pastoral care deals with all of these relationships. Regardless
of the nature of the presenting problem, from a theological perspective all counseling problems have to do with the brokenness
of at least one of these relationships. The solution to the problem
is normally found through the establishment of another relationship, the relationship between the caregiver and the care receiver.
Pastoral care is not accomplished without the establishment of
this very important trust relationship.

Because God chose the relationship between man and Christ
to be the means of salvation, the quality of pastoral care depends
on the quality of this restored relationship. Thus the emphasis of
real care changes from solving problems to creating meaningful
relationships. Problem solving happens in and through relationships.

The manifestation of God in Jesus Christ is important to the
caring person, because it is through the cross that we have the
answer to the problem of damaged relationships. Christ reconciled man back to God to reestablish man's most important relationship: "But as many as received him, to them gave he power
to become the sons of God, even to them that believe on his
name" (Jn 1:12). By making us part of his body, and by exhorting us to love one another, Christ became mankind's only hope
to bridge the gap between human and human. By making us
children of God, he has made us brothers and sisters. Then, by
giving humans power to be full persons, he reconciled man's
problem with man's own self.

In order to care adequately, through meaningful pastoral care
relationships, the caregiver needs certain qualifications. The first
is a *desire* to care. If someone does not have a genuine concern
for others and their needs and problems, they find genuine caring

nearly impossible. No technique will make a person genuinely care. This kind of love comes from the heart. It is a gift of God; it is a fruit of the Spirit (Gal 5:22, 23).

Ingredients of Caring

There are various "ingredients" that go with caring. M. Mayeroff's classic *On Caring*[86] lists some of these:

Discernment

A major ingredient of caring is discernment, which is the biblical equivalent of "knowing" or "understanding." Webster defines *discernment* as "the quality of being able to grasp and comprehend what is obscure ...." Discernment may call for skill and accuracy.

There is a classic story in the first book of Samuel that illustrates how a lack of discernment has made many pastors less effective. Eli was a respectable priest. There came to him a woman named Hannah who had a lot of problems at home. She was carrying a lot of pain. Finally she poured out her heart at the altar in the temple. Eli the priest watched the lady closely; he thought she was drunk. So he said to her, "How long will you keep on getting drunk? Get rid of your wine!" (1 Sam 1:14). He rapidly examined her symptoms and made a diagnosis—drunkenness—and gave her a prescription: "Dry up!" Hannah responded, "Not so, my Lord, I am a woman deeply troubled. I have not been drinking wine or beer; I was pouring out my soul to the Lord. Do not take your servant for a wicked woman; I have been praying here out of my great anguish and grief" (1 Sam 1:15, 16). Hannah's agony was amplified by the feeling of not being understood.

Understanding comes from listening very carefully to the other. Although listening is associated primarily with sounds, one must listen to more than the sounds to fully understand

---

86   M. Mayeroff, *On Caring* (New York: Harper and Row, 1971).

another person's pain. I believe this highly attentive listening
improves discernment.

Listening to Stories

Attentive, caring listening involves listening to "stories." It is
easy to understand others better through the stories they share
about themselves. Pastoral caregivers should encourage people
to tell their stories; it is only through those personal stories that
one person is revealed to the other. If someone says, "I am
suffering from phobia," I really do not understand what he is
talking about, but if I have him tell a story, I have a better opportunity to understand his problem.

Stories are extremely important to human communication. We
structure our memories and even our cognitive thought patterns
in story form. Jesus constantly used stories to communicate
truths, in several layers or at several levels.

Because our stories play such an important part in our lives,
pastoral caregivers should give more attention to stories than to
diagnostic labels. There seems to be a tendency for pastoral
counselors and caregivers to diagnose and label people too
rapidly, and often incorrectly. Consider the experience of David
when he found himself in the hands of the enemy. "So he pre-
tended to be insane in their presence; and while he was in their
hands he acted like a madman, making marks on the doors of the
gate and letting saliva run down his beard" (1 Sam 21:13). It is
easy to give this description of symptoms a very appropriate
label, but where lies the real story? Here is a man in fear for his
own life. He is under the most severe form of stress, and his
behavior is an attempt to cope with the situation. His desire is to
get out of the danger zone. There is always a story behind such
behavior. When we listen to a person's story, we understand
more fully and become able to care more accurately.

One woman was trying to explain to me that she has been suffering from a "fear for life." I did not comprehend the depth of
her pain or fear until she shared with me her story. This woman
was never able to show anger toward her husband. He always

threatened that if she ever got mad at him, he would kill himself. She tried her best to keep her feelings to herself, and succeeded for a long time, but finally she did have an argument with him. That night after they had gone to bed he got up and took an overdose of pills, ending up in the hospital. Although initially I could not understand her "fear for life," her "story" gave me a clear picture of her pain.

Patience

Another key ingredient of caring is patience, which Mayeroff defines not as waiting passively for something to happen, but as a kind of participation with the other in which we give fully of ourselves. Patience falls very close to hope and expectation.

Honesty

Honesty is another key ingredient of caring; people expect caregivers to be both genuine and honest. Pastoral caregivers, as men and women of God, should be honest with themselves first, and then honest with others as well. To tell the truth with love is not judgment; it is not rejection. It can be a true form of caring. God is in the business of making *new* people, not just *nice* people. We cannot help to renew people unless we tell the truth, in love.

Humility

In order to care, one also has to have a humble spirit. Being humble enough to learn from the other person makes us better caregivers. Pastoral care is not one-way traffic; there is something real the caregiver receives in return. It may be gratitude, affection, respect, or deepened understanding. There is always something that we can learn, or need to learn, from the other person. Recognizing and appreciating this is humility.

Healing

These days we talk much about healing without defining what we mean by that term. Many of us may think of healing as just the eradication of illness, but I believe healing can provide more than the absence of illness. Real health is an awareness of the presence of God, as well as the absence of illness. One definition of health may even be "the presence of the Lord." For a Christian, health is the process of living continually in the assurance that "even when I walk through the valley of the shadow of death, Thou art with me."

Ways of Caring

Sermons

There are many ways to express care. For pastors, preaching is a unique form of communicating care. One can reach out and touch many a hurting heart through "situational sermons." In one of my sermons I spoke of the wind that followed Noah's flood. The wind probably was violent, and may not have been welcomed by the family of Noah. If it had not been for that wind, however, where would their ark have been when the dry land appeared? They might have ended up floating around some ocean without an oar or a sail! There are times in our lives when our "ship" faces strong winds, but it may be that same fear-provoking wind that will bring us to the safety of dry land. I heard many comments about that sermon's comforting impact on members of my congregation, and realized that preaching can be used as an effective tool of caregiving, touching and encouraging many hearts.

Visitation

Pastoral care is demonstrated also through visiting the sick and needy. Most pastors agree that it is practically impossible to keep up-to-date on visitations; the load of administrative work on a pastor is often so heavy that he or she can hardly catch up. Yet visitation is actually a minister's privilege, and should not be ignored. No other professional is able to visit people without an invitation. We get to see people as they live. A phone call can also be a means of pastoral care, in some cases a better one. Very often troubled persons will call the pastor, and other times the pastor can make the call, particularly when he or she is unable to pay a visit in person. Lay pastors can and should be trained to assist in this vital form of caregiving.

Other Ways

Other ways of caring include:

• Designed group process,

• Individual and group Bible studies,

• Educational discussions,

• Devotional reading and listening, and

• Prayer

Appropriate small groups can be developed in churches and institutions. People who share common problems can be asked to meet with a facilitator for sharing and processing. This experience can be therapeutic to all participants without necessarily calling the groups "therapy groups."

Study of God's Word can be a powerful healing experience. Caregivers can encourage Bible study individually and in groups. Relevant Bible study outlines can be designed for particular needs and situations. God's Word can provide insights and revelation to enhance the healing of persons.

Teaching can be a way of caring. Topics of concern can be taught and discussed with individuals and groups. Experts can be invited to address relevant topics through Sunday School and adult education programs in churches.

Assigning devotional reading and listening is an appropriate way of offering care. Caregivers can ask people to keep a journal and allow them to share meaningful reflections with the caregiver. Therapeutic discussions can follow such experiences.

Praying for people communicates our ultimate care for them in the Name of Jesus. God is our source of healing and answers.

Praying for persons and their concerns and needs is a noble way
to minister care to individuals. In that sense, prayer is the ultimate ministry intervention.

Hazards

Pastoral care, like most worthwhile activities, has its hazards.
One hazard is pastoral over-confidence, which can prevent the
pastor from making careful referrals. Under-confidence is another hazard which affects many pastors. Yet another hazard is
the exploitation of pastors by attention-seeking parishioners, who
may take advantage of the pastor's unwillingness to turn them
down. Many pastors suffer from what could be called the "No
'No' Syndrome."

Pastoral care can leave the uncomfortable feeling of unfinished business. An institutional chaplain's caregiving begins
when the patient arrives and ends, in most cases, when the
patient is discharged; a local pastor is called upon at the onset of
the crisis, whether illness or other, and he or she remains a
resource throughout the crisis. A local pastor remains available
even after the crisis during the resolution of feelings. I often
found myself living with this unfinished feeling during my local
pastorate. In a fair-sized parish, it can be hazardous for a pastor
to live with that level of availability.

Uniqueness of Pastoral Care

Pastoral care is a unique ministry, one that should not be confused with any other helping profession. Howard Stone identified ten "theses" that emphasize the uniqueness of pastoral
care,[87] paraphrased here:

---

87 Howard W. Stone, *The Word of God and Pastoral Care* (Nashville:
    Abingdon, 1988), 25-27.

1. Pastoral care recognizes Christian resources.

2. Pastoral care does not seek to change an individual's personality.

3. A pastoral caregiver is not and cannot be a morally or theologically neutral person. It is not only acceptable but essential to have clear moral and theological convictions, which one must own and confess appropriately.

4. Pastoral work occurs in the context of the Christian community. Its identification with the pastoral office requires some tangible connection with the community of faith.

5. Pastoral care considers the priesthood of all believers.

6. Pastoral care cannot ignore systemic evil. It has a social orientation.

7. Pastoral care is not necessarily pastoral counseling. Pastoral care may lead to short-term pastoral counseling, but one can care without necessarily offering counseling. One cannot counsel, however, without caring.

8. Pastoral care is not reactive, it is proactive.

9. A pastoral caregiver does not deal just with feelings and attitudes. He or she also deals with beliefs, behaviors, and thinking processes.

10. Pastoral care is a preventive ministry. It deals with the "here and now" much more than with a person's history.

Pastoral care is a ministry of hope; thus, a pastoral caregiver is a hope-bearer. Andrew Lester reminds us that much of human suffering stems from hopelessness and futurelessness. He encourages us to assess the negative future stories of people and offer them a replacement vision of hope, framed in faith.[88]

---

88 Andrew D. Lester, *Hope in Pastoral Care and Counseling* (Louisville: Westminster, 1995).

William Hulme encourages the hope-bearing minister to be mindful of practical resources such as Scripture, faith, counseling skills, prayer, sacraments, and the community of faith.[89]

Obviously pastoral caregiving is hard work emotionally, but it is a privilege to be a caregiver in the Name of Christ. Adequately exercising this privilege requires theological perspective, practical wisdom, and psychological skills, but above all, love.

---

89   Hulme, *Pastoral Care and Counseling.*

4

The Psychological Side of Pastoral Care

The word "psychology" turns some Christians off, just as the word "theology" turns some psychologists off. Both groups have their own reasons for such a response. Psychological wisdom was around long before Sigmund Freud; it just was not called "psychology" in those days. (A more accurate and comprehensive term would be useful as we consider some of the ways modern psychology confirms biblical wisdom.)

The words of Jesus, and the writings of the apostles and church fathers, are rich in psychological wisdom. Thomas Oden has shed light on much of this wisdom in his *Pastoral Theology*.[90] Just as the atheist has his own distorted version of theology, it seems the anti-psychologists have their own somewhat distorted version of psychology. Ministers should not disregard all psychological wisdom just because modern psychologists have discovered and restated some of those truths. All truth originates in God, and therefore belongs to his church. Where psychologists have described new insights about the human self,

---

90 Oden, *Pastoral Theology.*

we ministers must not hesitate to use those insights to help humanity, wherever they do not contradict the Word of God, and whenever we can adopt them without violating our Christian convictions.

Pastoral care involves the inner self of a person. Psychology also attempts to deal with this area. How much psychology should a Spirit-filled pastor use in the practice of pastoral care? Let me share an example from a personal perspective, by sharing my own first encounter with the field of psychology.

Early in my seminary education, before I had any Clinical Pastoral Education training, I was introduced to the writings of Carl Rogers. I was immediately impressed with many of the concepts he was proposing.

Relationship

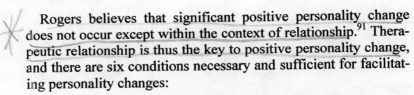

Rogers believes that significant positive personality change does not occur except within the context of relationship.[91] Therapeutic relationship is thus the key to positive personality change, and there are six conditions necessary and sufficient for facilitating personality changes:

1. Two persons are in psychological contact.

2. The first, whom we shall term the "client," is in a state of incongruence, being vulnerable or anxious.

3. The second person, whom we shall term the "therapist," is congruent or integrated in the relationship.

4. The therapist experiences unconditional positive regard for the client.

---

91 Carl Rogers, "The Conditions of Change from a Client-Centered View Point" in *Sources of Gain in Counseling and Psychotherapy*, edited by B. Berenson and R. Carkhuff (New York: Holt, Rinehart and Winston, 1967), 73.

5. The therapist experiences an empathetic understanding of the client's internal frame of reference and endeavors to communicate this experience to the client.

6. The communication to the client of the therapist's empathic understanding and unconditional positive regard is to a minimal degree achieved.[92]

Congruence

Congruence is very important within a therapeutic relationship. This means that the therapist, or helper, is real with the client. The helper is genuine, integrated, and authentic. A good helper does not have a bad "front." He or she can own, express, and accept negative feelings. He facilitates communication at all levels.

A good helper does not have to be a fully actualized person himself. He may not be "fully authentic," but he must be congruent in the relationship. In other words, he must be in the process of becoming himself.

Acceptance

A good helper offers unconditional positive regard and acceptance to his client. The helper is not possessive of the client. The more caring offered by the helper, the more successful the therapy will be. Acceptance is the recognition that the client has the right to have feelings; it is not the approval of all behavior. Rogers acknowledges that the helper cannot offer unconditional acceptance all the time; but this must be a "reasonably frequent ingredient."

Empathy

Accurate empathy is also very important for successful helping, according to Rogers. Empathy is a deep and subjective understanding of the client, of being *with* the client. Empathy is a sense of identification with the client. The counselor draws from

---

92 Ibid.

his or her own past to accomplish this. Emphasis is given to the here-and-now of the relationship. Like congruence and acceptance, empathy exists on a continuum.

Biblical Concepts

Rogers' ideas truly caught my attention, because until then I had been more familiar with methods of helping others that were either authoritarian ("God's Word says so"), judgmental ("You will go to hell"), or uninvolving ("We will pray about it, brother"). Rogers' proposals seemed like a breath of fresh air to me. I attempted to examine them biblically myself, and soon found my own reasons for adapting Rogers' major themes.

One of my major reasons for adapting Rogers' work for my own use is that I found unconditional positive regard and acceptance to be profoundly biblical concepts. God in Christ revealed that kind of acceptance for all of us, and Jesus manifested this quality throughout his life and ministry.

Jesus was a person-centered helper. He was always concerned about individuals. Whether that individual was the woman at the offering box or the man under the tree, Jesus had time for the individual. Who among the disciples could forget his focused attention on the woman of simple faith who was healed of continual bleeding!

It seemed to me that Jesus gave the first talk on congruence. Was not this his main message to the Pharisees? Jesus insisted on consistency. Within the individual and in society, He would not tolerate incongruencies.

The idea of giving authority to others is also biblical. Jesus taught that by giving, one receives. He taught that the best way to gain one's life is to lose it. When Jesus asked the man, "Do you want to be healed?," was Christ not giving that man responsibility for his own healing, in the sense that the man had the personal authority to choose his response? The man was healed by his correct response to Christ's offer. With all our teaching, coaching, and guiding, we may not heal anyone against his or her own will.

Rogers' idea of life as a process also seemed biblical to me. This is indeed a predominant theme in Paul's writings; he exhorts the believers again and again to make progress. Paul admonishes them to give up their childish ways and encourages them to press on toward the mark. He confesses that he has not arrived himself, but indicates that he is actively involved in growing and moving forward. Peter also exhorts his readers to "grow in grace and the knowledge of our Lord," and the writer of Hebrews reminds his readers that they must get rid of weights that so easily beset them.

Although I was greatly impressed with Rogers' concepts, and adapted the idea of unconditional positive regard as a basic tenet of my biblical approach to pastoral care, I was still unable to see psychological ideas as integral parts of a theology of pastoral care. Thomas Oden's *Kerygma and Counseling* helped me establish this connection. He has shown that there is an *implicit* assumption hidden in Rogerian psychotherapy which is made *explicit* in the Christian proclamation. Based on Karl Barth's doctrine of faith analogy, Oden demonstrated a relationship between a psychotherapeutic theory of human self-disclosure and a theology of God's self-disclosure.

Oden's proposal of this relationship between theory and theology seemed like the missing concept I was searching for. I was not violating the sacred by adapting some of Rogers' secular approach into my theory of pastoral care. As Oden said, "it is possible by means of the analogy of faith to perceive christologically the so-called secular counseling situation as the arena of God's self-disclosure."[93]

Hence, a new definition: *Acceptance* "refers to the source of self-affirmation in psychotherapy that is mediated through the

---

93 Thomas C. Oden, *Kerygma and Counseling* (Philadelphia: Westminster, 1966), 17.

counselor, and according to the Christian kerygma, made known
in history in the Christ event."[94]

As I am writing this, I am acutely aware (as was Oden) of the
fact that I am attempting to conjoin a humanistic therapy (the
presupposition that humans have within themselves the capacity
for appropriate self-direction), with a theology of revelation (the
assumption that the possibility for authentic existence comes to
man as a gift, mediated once for all through the self-disclosure of
God in Jesus Christ). This is a difficult task, yet Oden's argument is strong enough for me to accept.

Oden presents the following relevant points:

1. Psychotherapy mediates an accepting reality, which is
   grounded in *being* itself (the counselor is not the source of
   acceptance—he only points to an acceptance that has its
   source beyond himself);

2. The accepting reality, in being itself, has disclosed itself in
   an event to which the Christian proclamation explicitly
   witnesses;

3. Thus the implicit ontological assumption of all effective
   therapy is made explicit in the Christian proclamation.[95]

I must point out that acceptance and unconditional positive
regard are only the beginning points of caregiving; they are certainly not the totality of pastoral care. I have found that Rogers'
approach alone rarely completes the job of helping others, especially those who have serious emotional and spiritual needs. In
this regard, I found myself agreeing with Rogers' major critics.

Howard Clinebell, in his *Contemporary Growth Therapies*,
believes Rogers' theory has major weaknesses, as follows:

Rogers underemphasizes the special dynamics within and between social systems. He does not emphasize that personal

94 Ibid.
95 Ibid., 24.

problems are rooted in and fed by their social contents. Rogers neglects the power dynamics of growth, which Adler and the radical therapists emphasize as crucial. Once a relationship is established, the therapist must start *doing* in addition to *being*. He or she must speak the truth in love through appropriate confrontation. People with manipulative personalities can sabotage passive therapists.[96]

Clinebell also believes Rogers lacks awareness of the ingenuity and the power of resistance to growth within human beings. People who are "locked into self-sabotaging, self-deluding defenses against having to change" do not "spontaneously flower" in accepting-caring-honest relationships. Many require something more than Rogers' "midwifery" model. Many need a more active, structured and educative approach. Says Clinebell, "It seems as if, in freeing himself from moralistic fundamentalism, [Rogers] dismissed any need for a depth understanding of human pathology, evil, and destructiveness."[97]

According to Clinebell, Rogers' approach is further weakened by the "subjective hyper-individualism" that he proposes. By totally delegating all authority to the client, Rogers might be helping some, but he may also be fostering narcissistic "*me*-ism" in others. Some people may need helpers who can be active, purposive re-educators, willing to teach, coach, and guide the client.

Above all other objections as far as pastoral counselors are concerned, Rogers' approach lacks a place for either explicit value reformation or for actively facilitating spiritual growth. (Rogers reportedly confessed to Paul Tillich his lack of any need for a spiritual dimension.)[98]

My own experiences suggest that Clinebell's critique is correct, in that more aggressive modes of pastoral care need to be

---

96 Howard Clinebell, *Contemporary Growth Therapies* (Nashville: Abingdon, 1981), 120-124.
97 Ibid., 122.
98 Ibid., 124. Brooks E. Holifield refers to this in his *A History of Pastoral Care in America*, 332.

added to Rogers' method, as appropriate. A more explicit spiritual dimension also needs to be added. Although Rogers might not approve of the changes, the good news is that additions to his basic approach are an open possibility.

Robert Carkhuff, Gerard Egan and others have added to Rogers' method the following dimensions:

1. Levels of empathy,

2. Counselor self-disclosure,

3. Immediacy,

4. Concreteness, and

5. Confrontation.[99]

Carkhuff and Egan argue that a basic level of empathy is not enough. Egan has proposed an "advanced empathic listening,"[100] or a stage two empathy, a move from the subjective level to the objective level of understanding. According to Egan, advanced empathic listening places demands on clients to look at themselves at a deeper level, and asks that they begin to consider resources available to them. Stage two empathy also involves counselor self-disclosure.[101]

Immediacy is a form of self-disclosure relating to the here-and-now of the therapeutic relationship. Egan called immediacy "direct, mutual talk."[102] Concreteness means being specific in discussing one's concerns, feelings, thoughts, and actions.[103] Carkhuff, Egan and others wrote that effectiveness includes developing the skill of confronting clients in a caring fashion.

---

99   Gerald Corey, *Theory and Practice of Counseling and Psychotherapy*, 2nd
     ed. (Monterey, CA: Brooks/Cole, 1982), 89.
100 Gerard Egan, *The Skilled Helper* (Pacific Grove, CA: Brooks/Cole, 2000),
     201.
101 Ibid., 207.
102 Ibid., 209.
103 Robert R. Carkhuff, *Beyond Counseling and Therapy* (New York: Holt,
     Rinehart and Winston, 1977), 13-14.

This is not an attack on the client; rather it is an invitation for people to take a closer look at discrepancies between attitudes, thoughts, or behaviors.[104]

These additions to Rogers' methodology are needed. I do believe in employing confrontation when appropriate. Most of my ministry in a nonclinical setting, however, involves supportive listening, crisis intervention, and short-term counseling. Most of the counseling happens informally, not with appointments or counseling contracts. In these short-term situations, acceptance, unconditional positive regard, empathy, creative dialogue, appropriate God-talk,[105] and prayer are the most frequently used tools. As far as the addition of a spiritual dimension is concerned, a Christian caregiver must be open with others about his commitment to Christ, his gift of salvation for all men, and his Spirit who heals, guides, sustains and instructs. Howard Stone has made it abundantly clear that *pastoral care is not value neutral.*[106]

Even from a psychological perspective, pastoral care primarily involves listening, which includes empathy, understanding, and comforting, which all involve unconditional love (*agape*).

Listening

Listening is the skill upon which all pastoral care is based. It seems to me that I listen to stories all day long; I am called to be an empathetic and supportive listener. According to Charles Gerkin's hermeneutical theory of pastoral counseling, the goal of counseling is not mere insight-gathering or behavioral change, but its goal is to find new meaning for old stories.[107] New meanings can lead to new insights, and can change behavior.

Gerkin presents pastoral counseling as a process of interpretation and reinterpretation of human experiences, within the

---

104 Egan, 215.
105 Hulme, 110.
106 Stone, 25-26.
107 Charles V. Gerkin, *The Living Human Document: Revisioning Pastoral Counseling in a Hermeneutical Mode* (Nashville: Abingdon, 1984).

framework of a *primary* orientation toward the Christian mode of interpretation, in dialogue with contemporary psychological modes of interpretation. What the pastoral counselor needs more than anything, therefore, is effective tools of interpretation. The pastoral counselor offers the Christian interpretation of experiences.

Gerkin sees the pastoral counselor as a listener to stories as well as a bearer of them. Seeing all stories as interpretations enables the pastoral counselor to free people in crisis from being caught between a hermeneutic of despair and a hermeneutic of hope and expectations.[108]

 This hermeneutical theory appeals to me as a Spirit-filled minister because of the two major contributions it makes. First, the hermeneutical theory has evangelical connotations. The new birth can certainly be seen as a way of seeing things differently, a way of finding new meaning. Gerkin acknowledges that counseling can be evangelistic, if the counselee is not already a member of the community of faith.[109] Clinebell had already endorsed this concept.

Whether or not they are identified by theological labels, major theological issues that lie at the heart of counseling are sin and salvation (reconciliation), guilt and forgiveness, judgment and grace, spiritual death and rebirth. In a real sense, rebirth to wider worlds of meaning and relationships is the ultimate goal of pastoral counseling. Counseling is then one effective response to the words of a young carpenter prophet, "You must be born again."[110]

Understanding

Gerkin's theory appeals to me also because of its affirmation of the work of the Holy Spirit in the process of pastoral coun-

108 Ibid., 33.
109 Ibid., 182.
110 Howard J. Clinebell, *Basic Types of Pastoral Counseling* (Nashville: Abingdon, 1966), 46.

seling.[111] Gerkin sees the work of the Spirit as being somehow unique in relation to pastoral counseling, as opposed to other forms of counseling. As a Spirit-filled minister, I am extremely interested in exploring this possible dimension of ministry.

Biblically speaking, unconditional love and understanding are closely related.

Agape understands: it bears all things, believes all things, hopes all things, endures all things. It projects itself phenomenologically into the sphere of reference of the neighbor's inner life and receives him, believes his Word about himself, hopes all things for him which he most truly hopes for himself, yearns with him in his authentic intentions, shares with him all things, and endures with him through his quiet afflictions.[112]

This is true ministry of understanding. Ideally, this is what pastoral care is supposed to be. The caregiver will find useful concepts in the writings of Erik Erikson and James Fowler. Erikson's theory of the "eight stages of man" can increase one's understanding of individuals in terms of their particular stages in life.[113] This theory gives a general perspective within which an individual's problems can be better understood. Fowler's *Stages of Faith* increases one's appreciation for Erikson, as this volume reveals similarities between developmental stages and faith stages (although the latter is independent of chronological age).[114]

Comforting

Pastoral care involves a great deal of comforting ministry, because pastors are dealing with sufferers. Paul defines *comforting* in II Corinthians 1:3-4 as follows:

1. God is the source of all comfort,

---

111 Gerkin, 180-181.
112 Oden, *Kerygma and Counseling,* 158.
113 Erik H. Erikson, *Childhood and Society,* 2d ed. (New York: W.W. Norton, 1964), 219-233.
114 James W. Fowler, *Stages of Faith* (San Francisco: Harper and Row, 1981).

2. We ourselves have been comforted by God, and

3. We are called and enabled to share with others who are
   afflicted the comfort with which we ourselves have been
   comforted by God.[115]

We give more than our own finite consolation, insight and
reassurance. We give that which we have received from God
freely. Because we have received from God supportive, caring,
understanding encouragement, we freely share this encouragement as it flows through us during our interactions with others.[116]
In letting this happen in and through us, we become partakers in
the Kingdom of God and participants in the "healing reality of
the accepting love of God."[117]

Chronic Suffering

Comforting is a very important ministry, particularly with the
chronic sufferers. Many of these people will share stories of loss
and grief. The grief is often unresolved, so pastoral care of these
persons involves comforting that includes giving them permission to express feelings. Some people seem to require this permission more than others, as their theology discourages the grief
process by equating the expression of grief with a lack of faith.

Consequences of Unresolved Grief

In light of our understanding of the consequences of unresolved grief, helping people with the grief process has significant
implications. Long before psychoneuroimmunology became a
common term, Edgar Jackson documented the fact that unresolved grief can cause emotional and physical ailments. He
believed that abnormal grief accounts for many symptoms,
including upper respiratory disturbances, nausea, vomiting,
congestion, fainting, vertigo, trembling, shivering, convulsions,

115 Oden, *Kerygma and Counseling,* 158.
116 Ibid., 160.
117 Ibid., 162.

disturbance of the menses, cramps, tics and pains, and sleeplessness.[118] He reported that furious hostility was another manifestation of unresolved grief.[119]

Jackson contended that feelings and emotions related to grief do not cease to exist just because they have been denied expression. In other words, the mere passing of time does not heal. When repressed, strong feelings of grief find detours into forms of expression that may be disruptive in life. According to Jackson, many illnesses can in some instances be traced to unwisely managed grief as a contributing cause. The list of such illnesses includes ulcerative colitis, diabetes, asthma, arthritis, and even cancer. To repress one's grief, then, is neither controlling the grief nor being "strong." Such grief pressed down at one point may explode as a serious illness or manifest itself as a personality change or social maladjustment.[120]

Jackson's argument is supported by others like David Switzer and Thomas Welu. In his book *The Minister as Crisis Counselor*, Switzer reports that physical and emotional illness can result from unresolved grief. He lists several studies to support his position, including Dr. Erik Lindemann's study of forty-one patients with colitis.[121] Welu says unresolved grief can produce self-destructive behavior, as well as physiological problems such as spastic or ulcerative colitis, asthma, or rheumatoid arthritis.[122] These insights can be very helpful to the pastoral caregiver.

All these writers agree that unresolved grief has a way of finding unhealthy physical or emotional channels of expression. Having been surprised by the number of hospital patients living with unresolved grief, I agree with these authors and support

---

118 Edgar N. Jackson, *Understanding Grief* (New York: Abingdon, 1957), 167.
119 Ibid., 168.
120 Edgar N. Jackson, *When Someone Dies* (Philadelphia: Fortress, 1973), 34.
121 David K. Switzer, *The Minister as Crisis Counselor* (Nashville: Abingdon, 1974), 138-143.
122 Thomas C. Welu, "Pathological Bereavement: A Plan for its Prevention" in *Bereavement: Its Psychosocial Aspects*, edited by Bernard Schoenberg, et al. (New York: Columbia University, 1975), 139-149.

Jackson's own recommendation for grief ministry. He recommends that normal counseling techniques be followed with careful observation, creative listening, a tentative diagnosis that becomes a working basis in the relationship, and a plan of action that may include referral, personal counseling, or group involvement.[123]

My work as a hospital chaplain profoundly increased my faith in theologically sound and clinically sharp pastoral care. I am convinced of the valuable contribution that a pastor can make to the healing of ill persons. I have worked with patients with cancer, chronic pain, and general medical problems, and have concluded that almost all physical symptoms can be diagnosed as potentially spiritual/emotional symptoms.

I have seen the introduction of spiritual freedom enhance physical healing on numerous occasions. Because a person's body, mind and spirit truly are deeply interrelated in ways that we do not fully understand, it is essential to recognize that supportive, relational, care-frontational, reality-oriented pastoral counseling and care can help make people whole. My passion in writing about my own learning process is to share my own glimpse of this possibility, hoping to encourage my brothers and sisters in Spirit-filled ministry to catch a vision of this potential.

Resources

In this chapter I have briefly examined only one school of psychology, namely humanistic psychology as seen in the work of Carl Rogers. There are several schools of psychology, such as behaviorism, rational emotive therapy, transactional analysis, and cognitive therapy, from which one can draw selected resources. I am convinced that caregivers committed to Christ can find ways of incorporating biblically confirmed psychological perspectives from the secular field without compromising their convictions.

---

123 Jackson, *Understanding Grief,* 184.

While there are sincere Christians (such as Jay Adams and Martin Bobgan) who believe that no credible integration of Christian faith with psychology is possible, there are many others (such as Ray Brock and Richard Dobbins) who believe that such integration is not only possible but necessary. By keeping my biblical accountability at the forefront of my explorations, I find myself able to choose from the schools of psychology wisdom that is compatible with biblical teachings.

One does not have to buy into the presuppositions of various schools of psychology in order to glean psychological insights and frames of reference that can help in the work of Christian caregiving. *Psychology is only a toolbox. It cannot be the foundation of Christian pastoral care practice.* Just as a missionary relies on secular discoveries when he or she uses an airplane to get to the mission field, we may use psychological discoveries to get to our destination in counseling.

Ultimately, Christian caregiving is our accurate communication of God's love. Psychology can provide us some tools that may help us deliver this message of love accurately. We have already seen the possibility of seeing caregiving as implicit proclamation of God's Word, as opposed to preaching, which is explicit declaration of the same Word. If a social science helps us to proclaim that Word more efficiently, I believe we should examine its usefulness in light of that Word.

Developing a Psychological Theory

The guidelines for developing a psychological theory for pastoral work presented in William Miller and Kathleen Jackson's *Practical Psychology for Pastors* are most helpful. They suggest the following approaches:

1. *Flexible*: A thinking style that is open to new information rather than assumption-bound, seeking the paradigm to fit the individual rather than forcing all individuals to fit into a single mold.

2. *Eclectic*: In the best sense, being willing to consider perspectives and intervention approaches from a broad range of sources.

3. *Practical*: Helping you to know what to do next.

4. *Pragmatic*: Choosing on the basis of helpfulness; interested in information and research on the relative effectiveness of a variety of approaches.

5. *Differential*: Changing with the individual's needs, rather than applying a single perspective or intervention approach to everyone.[124]

Conclusion

In this chapter I have attempted to share the story of my personal encounter with psychology, hoping it demonstrates that pastors can work with *biblically scrutinized* psychology without selling out to secular psychology.

I am convinced that a minister can benefit from psychology without violating his call or conscience. Just as a modern missionary benefits from secular high-tech tools such as mass communication and jet airplanes, a modern pastor can enhance his or her ministry effectiveness by using ancient and modern psychological insights.

---

124 William R. Miller and Kathleen A. Jackson, *Practical Psychology for Pastors* (Englewood Cliffs, NJ: Prentice-Hall, 1995), 86.

5

Assessment in Pastoral Care

Physical and emotional problems lead modern man to seek professional help in the medical world. Persons presenting physical and emotional symptoms bring with them many unmet spiritual needs of which they may not even be aware. Persons engaged in pastoral care ministry must develop skills in assessing the spiritual needs of their clients.

Pastoral care is a ministry of giving. In this ministry the giving must match the needs of the receiver; therefore, caregiving is most effective and appropriate when it follows a process of assessment. Pastoral caregivers thus need to develop skills in assessment and spiritual diagnosis.

Need for Assessment

People engaged in spiritual care ministry can learn much from the medical profession. Physicians deal with medical problems in stages. Several stages of medical treatment are assessment, diagnosis, development of a care plan, and implementation. This assessment model may be valuable for use by pastoral caregivers as well.

Physicians are trained not to assume or guess, but to act only after making careful observations and measurements. Even when dealing with crisis, physicians do not "shoot everything that moves." They do not prescribe without first observing and assessing.

Unfortunately, people engaged in ministry often begin spiritual "treatment" without prior assessment or pause for discernment. We must remember that Jesus did not give the same treatment to everyone. He dealt with the Samaritan woman in one way; he dealt with the woman caught in adultery in a different way. The blind men were treated one way; the man who was lowered through the roof was treated another way. Jesus knew what Martha needed; he knew the different need of Zacchaeus. Jesus always seemed to assess the true need of the individual before he responded.

Proper spiritual assessment can prevent unnecessary hardship on the individual and possible embarrassment for the minister. Caregivers who fail to make proper assessment tend to offer their favorite spiritual exercise as a solution for all spiritual problems.

Spiritual assessment requires both observation and discernment. The Bible teaches us that the individuals' descriptions of their need do not always reflect their real needs. For example, in 2 Kings 4 the wife of the prophet described her need as financial, yet the prophet gave her oil, not money. In 1 Kings 19:4, when Elijah thought his need was sudden death, the Lord did not consider that to be his real need. In Acts 3 the lame man at the Beautiful Gate thought his need was for economic assistance, but the apostle offered him physical healing instead. At the well, the

Samaritan woman's true need was not a new marriage; she needed the living water! Discernment enables a caregiver to make proper assessment of true spiritual needs before responding.

Discernment is not a substitute for inquiry. Discernment complements observation and inquiry. This chapter deals with the issue of pastoral assessment.

Stages of Life

Individual needs of persons are related to their stages of life. Erik Erikson can teach us much about these stages from a psychosocial perspective. He described eight stages in a person's life, each marked by a specific developmental crisis. In a healthy growth process, people who successfully resolve each crisis grow and move to the next stage. Those who have been unable to successfully resolve the life-stage crisis, however, move to the next stage with unresolved issues from the previous one.

Erikson determines the eight stages of life by these life crises, or conflicts:

1. Basic Trust vs. Mistrust

2. Autonomy vs. Shame/Doubt

3. Initiative vs. Guilt

4. Industry vs. Inferiority

5. Identity vs. Role Confusion

6. Intimacy vs. Isolation

7. Generativity vs. Stagnation

8. Integrity vs. Despair[125]

---

125 Erik H. Erikson, *Childhood and Society.*

A person's stage of life becomes, then, a valuable clue to his or her developmental needs. For instance, the issue of greatest concern for an adolescent is *identity*. The issue for a young adult is *intimacy*. The clue to assessing the crisis issue in the life of a senior adult would be *integrity*.

Each stage of life demands its own developmental tasks. An understanding of these developmental tasks can point the caregiver to special pastoral care needs. Havighurst has divided adulthood into three periods, listing the developmental tasks in each of these periods:

Early Adulthood (ages 18 to 30)

- Selecting a mate

- Learning to live with a marriage partner

- Starting a family

- Rearing children

- Managing a home

- Getting started in an occupation

- Taking on civic responsibility

- Finding a congenial social group

Middle Age (ages 30 to 55)

- Selecting a mate

- Achieving adult civic and social responsibility

- Establishing and maintaining an economic standard of living

- Assisting teenage children to become responsible and happy adults

- Developing adult leisure-time activities

- Relating to one's spouse as a person

- Accepting and adjusting to the physiological changes of middle age

- Adjusting to aging parents

Later Maturity (ages 55 and over)

- Adjusting to decreasing physical strength and health

- Adjusting to retirement and reduced income

- Adjusting to death of a spouse

- Establishing an explicit affiliation with one's age group

- Meeting social and civic obligation

- Establishing satisfactory physical living arrangements[126]

Maturational Needs of Adults

Specialists in adult education have attempted to categorize the maturational needs of adults, identifying some of the universal dimensions of maturation. The process of maturation involves moving from one state of being to another.[127]

Moving from...........................Toward

Dependence ....Autonomy
Passivity ....Activity
Subjectivity ....Objectivity

---

126 Robert J. Havighurst, *Developmental Tasks and Education* (New York: David Makay Company, 1961), 72-98.
127 Malcolm S. Knowles, *The Modern Practice of Adult Education* (New York: Cambridge/The Adult Education Company, 1980), 29.

Ignorance.................................Enlightenment
Small abilities..........................Large abilities
Few responsibilities ....Many responsibilities
Narrow interests.....................Broad interests
Selfishness..............................Altruism
Self-rejection...........................Self-acceptance
Amorphous self-identity ....Integrated self-identity
Focus on particulars...............Focus on principles
Superficial concerns...............Deep concerns
Limitation...............................Originality
Need for certainty ....Tolerance for ambiguity
Impulsiveness.........................Rationality

Hierarchy of Needs

Human needs are multi-dimensional and hierarchical. Abraham Maslow developed a hierarchy of human needs based on the concept that individuals must have their lower level needs met before they can pay attention to their higher level needs. This concept is very important for caregivers.

In Maslow's model, the physiological or survival needs are on the first, or most basic, level of need. Safety needs are the next level to be met, then the need for love and belonging. The need for self-esteem is the next level; the need for self-actualization is at the highest level. While the most basic needs have to do with survival physically and psychologically, the highest need has to do with self-fulfillment, which from a Christian perspective can be identified as "fullness of life," or "Kingdom lifestyle."[128]

---

128 Ibid., 28.

Whole Person Assessment

Needs assessment in pastoral care must look at and beyond developmental needs. An individual's needs as a whole person must be considered. The spiritual care staff at Oral Roberts University developed an instrument to assess these. This tool, called the Whole Person Assessment, was developed from several sources. Based on one or more interviews, the spiritual care staff was able to develop a profile of a person's "whole-person needs." A pastoral care plan was then developed based on the Whole Person Assessment, condensed below:

Whole Person Assessment

I. Spiritual Assessment

    A. Patient's Relationship with God

    B. Patient's Relationship with the Local Church

    C. Patient's Understanding of Prayer, Medicine & Healing

II. Personal Events/Changes during the Past Few Years

III. Emotional Dimension

IV. Marital Relationship

V. Family/Household Events

VI. Vocational Events

VII. Financial Condition

VIII. Pastoral Care Plan

Unique Aspects

Although needs assessment is a form of diagnosis, pastoral assessment of needs is different from medical diagnosis. In pastoral assessment, one is dealing with the individual as an epistle, as Paul used the term, or as a living human document, as Boisen proposed. Assessment then is not simply a matter of subjective and objective observations, but a hermeneutical exercise as well. The minister is engaged in reading and interpreting the epistle or the spiritual document that is the person.

Purpose of Pastoral Assessment

The purpose of pastoral assessment is not to "pin down" a diagnosis as if the person were a lifeless object.[129] It is not to find out what someone *has*, but rather to find out what they *are*. The purpose of pastoral assessment has been described as follows:

1. To care more accurately for the pains and possibilities,

2. To deepen the patient's self-understanding,

3. To know in a deeper, more meaningful way,

4. To enable the person to know *self* in relation to *problem*,

5. To enable the person to know *self* in relation to *others*, and

6. To shed light on how God is involved in our experiences of pain and hope.[130]

---

129 Steven S. Ivy, "Pastoral Diagnosis is Pastoral Caring," *Journal of Pastoral Care* 42, no. 1 (spring 1988), 81-89.
130 Ibid.

Five Key Questions

There are five key questions a caregiver must ask in order to ascertain the unique needs of an individual:

1. Why is this person telling me this now?

2. What is troubling this person?

3. What is causing the problem?

4. What is missing?

5. What is needed?[131]

The first question, which is not often asked directly, can be asked in at least five different ways by the simple method of mentally changing the emphasis each time:

1. *Why* is this person telling me this now?

2. Why is *this person* telling me this now?

3. Why is this person *telling me* this now?

4. Why is this person telling me *this* now?

5. Why is this person telling me this *now*?

When this complex first question has been thus thoroughly applied, the caregiver moves closer to the real needs of the individual involved. Then the caregiver gathers the information yielded by the answers to the other four questions.

Pastoral assessment, when properly done, deals with several themes in the life of the person concerned. Several models exist for examining themes.

---

131 Ibid.

Donald Capp's Model

Donald Capp presents a model with three themes:

1. Interest and intentions

2. The structural personality

3. Interaction between individual and social environment[132]

Dan McKeever's Model

Dan McKeever presents yet another model, with five interpretive keys:

1. Suffering/hurting patterns

2. Covenant/commitment capacity

3. Binding/freeing components

4. Identity projections

5. Reality foci[133]

Paul Pruyser's Themes

Paul Pruyser, in his *Minister as Diagnostician*, challenges ministers to use theological language and concepts to make theological diagnoses.[134] Pruyser contributes seven theological themes to help the minister in this work of assessment:

1. Awareness of the Holy,

2. Sense of providence,

3. Stance of faith,

---

132 Ibid.
133 Ibid.
134 Paul W. Pruyser, *The Minister as Diagnostician* (Philadelphia: Westminster Press, 1978).

4. Experiences of grace or gratefulness,

5. Process of repenting,

6. Feeling of communion, and

7. Sense of vocation.

I find these themes helpful in doing interpretive work with the personal stories I hear as a caregiver.

Serious Mental Illness

The National Mental Health Association (NMHA) has produced the following list of signs of serious mental illness for use by clergy. Caregivers will want to be familiar with these signs as they do their work of pastoral assessment. It is important that ministers understand these recommendations of the NMHA.

Ten Signs of Serious Mental Illness

1. Big changes in behavior

2. Periods of confusion/loss of memory

3. Thinks people are plotting against self/has grandiose ideas about self

4. Talks to self/hears voices

5. Thinks people are watching/talking about him or her

6. Visual hallucination/odors/tastes

7. Complaints about impossible bodily changes

8. Performs repetitive acts/flight of ideas

9. Depression

10. Dangerous to self/others

The NMHA has provided an abridged version of the explanation of these symptoms, with additional instructions for clergy:

Explanation of Symptoms

The person who shows signs of emotional difficulties is letting those around him know that he is ill and troubled. His illness is his way of dealing with intense problems that are too painful, too confusing, too demanding, or too filled with decisions and challenges.

1. *He shows big changes in his behavior.* This may be noted, for example, in a person who has always been a serious, respected member of the community but who suddenly becomes quite quarrelsome, stays out late at night, or gambles with a group with whom he never before had any association. Or he may become persistently antagonistic, get into frequent fights or, on the other hand, become unusually happy for no apparent reason. He may even become so preoccupied with apparently unimportant matters that he is too busy to eat or sleep.

2. *He has strange periods of confusion or loss of memory.* All of us go through fleeting moments of being forgetful about the day or week, or we are unable to recall the name of a friend. The psychotic person, however, may repeatedly forget who he is, that he is married, or what day or month it is. He may even have difficulty in telling you where he is now or where he was a few days ago. (This may instead be a symptom of the onset of degenerative brain disease such as Alzheimer's.)

3. *He thinks people are plotting against him or has grandiose ideas about himself.* The mentally ill person may believe that the people with whom he works are plotting to get him fired, and he may become very aggressive towards these fellow employees because of such unfounded thoughts. He may also think that persons he does not even know are plotting against him. Or he may believe all activities in a factory would cease if he missed one day's work, even

though his job is quite simple and his absence would not at all affect the smooth operation within the factory.

4. *He talks to himself and hears voices.* Many people on occasion talk quietly to themselves when they are alone. However, the psychotic person may talk vigorously to himself even though there are many people around him. He may tell you with the utmost sincerity that he is responding to a voice that is talking solely to him. Some persons having these experiences may suddenly stare off into the distance, or they may interrupt a conversation or an activity to respond to the voice that they hear. Bringing to the ill person's attention that there are no such imaginary voices will do no good. He may persist in hearing these voices and may vehemently resist the suggestion that it is just his imagination.

5. *He thinks people are watching him or talking about him.* In the early phases of some mental illness, the person may be quite sensitive and feel that his movements are being watched, and that the people in the community discuss him.

6. *He sees things, smells strange odors, or has peculiar taste experiences.* These symptoms are usually related to the five principal senses – hearing, seeing, tasting, smelling and feeling. The mentally ill person may have irrational reactions to what his senses are experiencing. This person may tell you that he sees things that you know do not exist, or he may tell you that there is a sickening odor in the room, or that he has a horrible taste in his mouth caused by poison being put in his food. Since these thoughts are very important to him, a rational attempt to prove them false is rarely adequate.

7. *He has complaints of bodily changes that are not possible.* He may think that his heart is actually not beating, or that he is suffering from a rare fatal illness. He may believe his face is disfigured or that he is immune to pain and other sensations.

8. *He suffers from the need to perform repetitive acts many times over, or is plagued by foreboding thoughts.* He may have a morbid fear of germs and spend an inordinate amount of time in such acts as hand washing every time he touches a book, a doorknob, a dollar bill, or any object handled by other people. Or he may be possessed with the terrible thought that he will do harm to a member of his family.

9. *He shows markedly depressed behavior.* Almost everyone at some time feels "blue" or discouraged. These are normal reactions, most often following some loss. The clergyman meets many such "normal" periods of discouragement in his ministry to the bereaved. However, some depressed persons are severely ill. They suffer from a far greater, more profound disruption of personality.

   He may feel utterly worthless and alone. He may sit for hours, not speaking or moving, with his head hung down in an air of complete dejection. He may actually give up hope and think of suicide. Unfortunately, a vacation from responsibility, rest, and even little kindnesses are more likely to aggravate than help.

10. *He behaves in a way that is dangerous to others.* The number of such instances is slight, but a mentally ill person may decide to hurt another person who he feels is persecuting him. An individual suffering from such a disorder may tell a convincing story of how he is being abused by another, even though there is repeated assurance that this person is in no way involved and could not possibly do such a thing; still the disturbed person is not convinced.

What the Clergy Can Do

Almost never is there any benefit for the clergyman to argue with or dispute heatedly the distortions of reality that a disturbed person may present. When the person has "lost contact with reality," skillful psychiatric help is needed to help him resume contact with those around him, and referral to a professional treatment source should be made.

When a member of the clergy becomes aware of individuals who show serious or prolonged signs of the symptoms cited above, he or she should get in touch with the person who is most properly concerned, usually a member of the family. The minister should then attempt to help the interested relative perceive that psychiatric care is indicated.

Frequently the relative is not able to accept the fact that someone close to him is mentally ill. He considers it a disgrace because he feels cultural shame about illnesses that affect the mind. In some instances, relatives may even have a need to deny the existence of mental illness because they fear that they are somehow the cause of the loved one's illness. However, the clergyman who is sensitive to the underlying reasons for their inability to accept a loved one's mental illness will work to find a way to help them accept the need for medical attention. In many instances, even after the relatives have accepted the need for psychiatric care, the clergyman may be asked to discuss the need for treatment directly with the mentally ill person. The relatives may be too involved emotionally to handle this major crisis effectively.

The first and most logical source of assistance is the disturbed person's physician. Where there is no particular physician, the clergyman may find help by calling the local medical society. The clergyman may not find it easy to help the mentally ill person obtain treatment. On many occasions, the ill person is too disoriented to discuss his need for treatment. In these instances, it will be necessary for the clergyman to ask a doctor, a social worker, or a person from one of the related professions to help the family in getting the patient to the appropriate treatment sources.

Fortunately, most of us do not run into serious mental illness very often. Also, we do not believe that mental illness is beyond God's healing power. God heals brokenness in all areas of our lives—body, mind, spirit, relationships, finances, etc.

Moving from Assessment to Planning for Care

Once the needs assessment has been done, the caregiver can develop a care plan to meet the particular needs revealed. There are various models one can adapt to move from assessment to planning. Miller and Jackson's model, for instance, involves:

1. Identification of the problem (need),

2. Reconstruction of the problem (listening, clarifying),

3. Diagnostic interpretation (mutual assessment), and

4. Intervention (plan, strategy).[135]

The caregiver may want to adopt this model or another model for sharpening the assessment process and developing a care plan.

Spiritual Assessment Model

The following spiritual assessment tool is one I developed based on Galatians 5:22-23 (the fruit of the Spirit). Individuals may rate themselves on the nine fruits of the Holy Spirit on a scale where 1 is the lowest score and 10 is the highest. A graph can be drawn based on the values marked by the individual. This can be used especially with married couples, as they can evaluate each other in these categories. This tool can be used to guide pastoral care and to monitor progress.

---

135 Miller and Jackson, *Practical Psychology for Pastors.*

Mathew's Model for Spiritual Assessment
Based on the Fruits of the Spirit in Galatians 5:22-23

1 = Low 10 = High		1	2	3	4	5	6	7	8	9	10
Love	Toward God										
	Toward Others										
	Toward Self										
Joy	In the Lord										
	In troubles										
	In relationships										
Peace	With the Lord										
	With self										
	With others										
Patience	In tribulation										
	With self										
	With others										
Kindness	Toward strangers										
	Toward relatives										
	Toward self										
Generosity	Toward needy										
	Toward family										
	Toward church										
Faithfulness	To God										
	To church										
	To others										
Gentleness	Toward weak										
	Toward strong										
	Toward self										
Self-Control	In body										
	In mind										
	In spirit										
1 = Low 10 = High		1	2	3	4	5	6	7	8	9	10

Developed by T.M. Mathew, D.Min., Ed.D.

6

A Clinical Model
of Care Ministry
for the Church

Pastoral care is a healing ministry, an extension of the healing ministry of Jesus. This ministry is not limited to hospital chaplaincy. All disciples of Jesus are called into the healing ministry of Jesus.

Members of the spiritual care staff at Oral Roberts University developed a model for pastoral care ministry called the Five-Fold Ministry of Healing. Volunteer lay chaplains and ORU. students were trained in this basic model of ministry. I share a simple outline of this clinical model in this chapter, with the suggestion that this clinical model is flexible enough to be adapted to the special needs of the local church. This model can become the heart of a lay ministry of pastoral care in the local church.

A Five-Fold Ministry of Healing

The five-fold ministry of healing involves:

1. Incarnational presence,

2. Listening,

3. Information gathering,

4. Counseling/Referral, and

5. Prayer.

(When lay trainees lack significant experience in counseling, that dimension must be omitted.)

1. Incarnational Presence

The ministry of incarnational presence is living in the realization that just being with a suffering person can help to bring about healing, or at least a greater ability to cope with pain and suffering. Being an incarnational presence does not require doing or talking. It only requires being with the sufferer. "Christ in you is the hope of glory" (Col 1:27).

2. Listening

There is a worldwide shortage of listeners and a surplus of talkers. Anyone who can listen with support, care and empathy adds great value to our lives. The human need to be heard is universal; unfortunately, the ability to listen is not as pervasive as the need to be listened to. Listening skills must be learned through concentration and much practice.

3. Information Gathering

Patients in hospitals usually reveal three types of information to the minister:

a. Information the *minister* can use to provide the patient with the needed spiritual and emotional care;

b. Information the *physician* can use to provide the patient with more thorough medical care;

c. Information the *nursing staff* can use to provide the patient with more thorough nursing care.

(Sometimes patients give their minister information relevant to medical care without realizing that it should have been given to their physician or nurse.)

A good pastoral care listener zeroes in on the patient's feelings, and not just the facts they share. Statements such as "I'm angry," "I'm tired of ...," "This is so painful to me," "I don't think anyone knows what's wrong with me," will be helpful clues to lead the minister to a deeper understanding of the patient's needs. It is usually the patient's feelings that tell you where prayer is needed in his or her life. Ministers must listen to *what* is being said and *who* is saying it. Good listeners ask themselves: Is this a frightened person? Are these an angry person's words? This type of listening is hard work, and it requires disciplined practice.

4. Referral

In a hospital situation, when the lay minister relays medical information to the patient's physician or nurse, he is performing the ministry of referral. The ministry of referral is valuable because it places information into the hands of the professionals best qualified to make therapeutic use of it for the patient, and it promotes an atmosphere of team harmony among ministers, physicians, nurses and other professionals.

At times the lay caregiver will encounter information about spiritual and emotional needs which may be too complex for a nonprofessional to handle. In such cases, the information must be relayed to the appropriate person under whom he or she is working.

5. Prayer

Prayer is the focus of this five-fold care ministry. When praying, the pastoral care minister should summarize the concerns the person has expressed. In so doing he demonstrates that he has listened with compassion and accuracy. The words of a prayer can minister realistic hope and affirmation to the needy person, in addition to conveying a petition to God.

Counterproductive Practices

Pastoral caregivers need to know that certain perceived practices are not helpful. Practices which are counter-productive to the five-fold pastoral care ministry include:

Debating Theological Ideas

Arguing with care-receivers, especially about religious doctrines, brings no good results because it produces strife that can remove the trust from the care-giving/receiving relationship. Overpersuasive efforts to convert clients may annoy them rather than causing them to accept Jesus Christ.

Advice-Giving

Those who believe they have a magical power to solve other people's complex problems will experience frustration in pastoral care ministry. The best approach is to be patient in giving persons caring support so that they can, with God's help, solve their own problems.

Giving advice is a risky business. Good advice might help someone temporarily, but constant advice-giving can cause dependence on the caregiver. Advice which turns out to be bad advice will cause problems for the patient. In this day and age even good advice which does not produce the desired result can generate lawsuits against caregivers. The safest and most productive approach is to engage in ministry where persons are assisted to discover solutions to their problems or experience divine intervention in their affairs.

Wrong Assumptions

A guarantee of instantaneous, total healing may result in disappointment or disillusionment for those who are seriously ill, should God instead heal them gradually, or ultimately in the resurrection. Although as God's servants it is our privilege to earnestly pray for total and complete healing of persons, we must never forget that God is our sovereign deciding the method and timing of healing.

Untrained Counseling

Counseling must be done by professional ministers who have the necessary training and experience. Volunteers must not attempt in-depth counseling.

Preaching During Counseling

Knowledge of doctrines and the Scriptures is desirable, but overwhelming displays of it tend to make care-receivers feel that they know too little Scripture to qualify for God's help in obtaining healing. Pastoral caregivers need to develop skills required to share God's Word in more meaningful ways. The Word can become flesh in more practical ways.

Self-Focus

Since pastoral care ministry is a person-centered ministry, the receiver's needs and interests must be kept uppermost. Ministers who often speak of their own experiences will not be effective in this ministry.

Unanswerable Questions

Attempts to answer unanswerable questions are always inadequate, and they usually put guilt on the person who asked the question. No one knows just why a particular person is not healed, or why there are such sorrows as AIDS, birth defects, natural disasters, or the suffering of the innocent. In pastoral care ministry, it is perfectly acceptable to say, "I don't know the answer to your question." These are questions that allow individuals to express their yearning to experience God's presence alongside them, even while the questions go begging theological solutions. *Allowing them to express their questions* is more therapeutic than trying to provide the answers.

Exorcism

Unless one is in a situation where no other believer is present but the action is immediately needed, pastoral care ministers encountering persons who appear to be demon-possessed, or say they are, should not attempt solo exorcism. This is a ministry in the realm of principalities and powers, requiring spiritual strength and preparation. Just as no neurosurgeon would attempt open brain surgery without a second opinion and considerable preparation, no wise minister will act hastily in such a situation. While there are times when the situation calls for immediate action, the normal mode of operation should be one of exercising caution and *involving prayer support*.

Harmony and Modesty

Volunteer lay ministers should minister in harmony with the teachings of the sponsoring church or ministry. Ministry by pastoral caregivers is most effective when done in a modest manner rather than a showy manner. It is good to maintain a "decreased" spirit as John the Baptist had (Jn 3:30).

Confidentiality

Violation of confidentiality of information about a client is the unpardonable sin of pastoral care ministry! Receive the care-receiver's consent before sharing even seemingly inconsequential details with others, unless life is at risk. Caregivers today must also take responsibility to familiarize themselves with their state's laws regarding confidentiality, child abuse reporting, etc., as they may be professionally subject to some of these regulatory provisions.

Effective Principles

A Teachable Spirit

Pastoral care ministers who bear in mind certain principles will develop a more effective approach to ministry. For example, a humble, teachable spirit is conducive to further growth. Persons who regard the ministry program as a growth opportunity are especially suited. This is true even of those who know nothing about ministry but want to learn.

Teamwork

Individuals who get fulfillment from being a member of a team are compatible with a pastoral care program. Anyone who has a drive to be a religious Superman or Wonder Woman would not adapt well to this ministry.

Self-Restraint

Persons who are restrained in their use of God's name as their authority for the things they say and do are more effective in pastoral care. People who frequently and casually mention God as inspiring everything they do seek to create the impression that they have a superior communication with God. Such individuals try to bolster their credibility by inappropriately invoking the authority of God on essential and nonessential matters. By doing so, they put everyone who disagrees with them in the position of challenging God. Often, ordinary people exhibiting this pattern are plagued with low self-esteem. They fear their opinions may not be accepted, so they present them as pronouncements from God.

Discretion in Touch

Touch and personal space are important in pastoral encounters. Many Christians regard touching as a natural expression of affection, but others may not. For that reason, pastoral care ministers must be discreet in their use of touch. It is proper to take the hand of a hurting person and say, "Do you have any concerns that I might pray about?" A light touch on the head, hand, upper back, or shoulder is always regarded as proper. Never touch bare skin except the hand. It is better never to hug anyone without permission.

Recognition of Personal Space

In a hospital or counseling situation, the effectiveness of the pastoral work may be canceled when the client's normal personal space is violated. A distance of two to four feet is close enough to convey intimacy without being threatening. Eye contact should be continuous in order to communicate that the client has your undivided attention, but your gaze should not be so intense that it makes him uncomfortable. *Never* sit on a hospital patient's bed.

Length of Visit

The length of a visit with a patient in the hospital is important. As a member of the healing profession, the pastoral care minister must be aware that physicians and nurses need adequate time to render patient care, and the patient may be wearied by lengthy visits.

No Personal Agenda

Finally, the pastoral visitor must bring no agenda of his own into an encounter with a care-receiver. It is his task to carry out the five-fold ministry in such a manner that will enable the person to express his needs and concerns, so those matters may be conveyed to the Lord in prayer. The minister should not guide the conversation toward topics of his own interest. He or she should instead help the patient verbalize the joys, sorrows, and problems that are uppermost in the patient's life at that time.

Improving Counseling Skills

The principles listed above are important for all types of caregiving. While I have de-emphasized counseling in this discussion because I believe that one can do caregiving without doing counseling, I do indeed believe that all caregivers should consciously seek to improve their counseling skills.

7

A Pastoral View
of Pain and Suffering

The problem of evil—the existence of pain and suffering—cannot be solved philosophically or theoretically. It is only within the individual experience that pain and suffering can be understood as transformational, good overcoming evil, in the life of a Christian person.

Pastoral care is the ministry of bearing one another's burdens (Gal 6:2, 5). This is a ministry involving ongoing encounters with those who are suffering. Having an adequate theology of pain and suffering is a prerequisite for good pastoral work. Suffering, however, is a difficult topic for Pentecostals and charismatics who believe in prayer and miracles.

As a pastor and hospital chaplain, I have worked among people who found themselves in the midst of conflict, pain and suffering. In spite of all the technological advances, hospitals still are full of pain and anguish. People struggle daily with very deep issues of life. These people ask many difficult questions, especially about their suffering. As ministers of the Gospel, we are confronted with these questions on many occasions. While we cannot or do not have the answers to many of these questions, it is critical that we each have a personal perspective on the problem of suffering.

I now realize that I do not have to answer these questions, but I am convinced that having a personal perspective on the problem of suffering is an important prerequirement for all caregivers.

Different versions of popular theology are available on the subject of suffering. While some believe that good Christians do not suffer at all, others deny their actual suffering. Some blame themselves or someone else for their suffering. Others blame God and resign themselves to agony.

What is the meaning of suffering? Is there a comprehensive Christian view of suffering? This chapter will present a variety of theories and perspectives and will conclude with a synthesis of this survey of the written materials. Thomas Oden presented an excellent review of the classical writers on the subject of suffering in his *Pastoral Theology;*[136] we will also review more recent writings.

Many brilliant minds have contemplated the problem of pain in the world. Indeed, pain is a difficult subject, and no one seems to have an answer that suits everyone. Arguments continue about pain as the foolishness of God, as opposed to the wisdom of God, yet the reality of pain in the world seems unaffected by these intellectual efforts to explain God. The Bible states that there will be pain in the world until God makes all things new (Revelation 21:4).

Although of course no one wants to experience pain, a biological examination of pain reveals its place and function in this world. Pain is a warning system. It demands a response. Pain causes us to withdraw our fingers from the stove, saving us from further harm. This revelation of the wisdom of God in the design of the pain system gives rise to Dr. Paul Brand's comment:

---

136 Oden, *Pastoral Theology.*

"Thank God for inventing pain! I don't think He could have done a better job."[137] Brand's sophisticated research confirmed the genius behind the pain system.

For someone with crippling arthritis or terminal cancer, a painless world would seem like heaven itself. However, the pain network performs daily protective service throughout our life-times. "Pain, then, is not God's great goof. It is a gift—the gift that nobody wants. Without it, our lives would be open to abuse and horrible decay."[138]

Let us look into a comprehensive biblical view of the subject of suffering presented in John Steely's translation of the book *Leiden*.[139] The Old Testament does not give a uniform interpreta-tion of suffering, because suffering appears in many different forms and poses riddles that are too difficult.[140] Man has a tre-mendous need to fit suffering into his understanding of the structure of the world in some meaningful way, but suffering remains ambiguous.[141] In Old Testament thinking, Israel's one God is ultimately responsible for all the good and the bad in the universe; the presupposition is that in some way the sufferer himself gives impetus to his suffering. The Old Testament writ-ers do not systematize the multiplicity of experiences, causes, and interpretations of suffering. They seem to take each calamity individually and attempt to deal with each pragmatically.

The Old Testament offers some comfort to the sufferer, in that the God of Israel suffers with his people. However, compared to the New Testament, it does not offer as a counter-balance to suffering a strong hope in the hereafter. This hope is offered when the New Testament completes the Old Testament. While the suffering of Jesus is central to the New Testament, the hope of resurrection, of life after death, provides a way to ultimately

---

137 Paul Brand, cited in Philip Yancey, *Where is God When It Hurts?* (Grand Rapids: Zondervan, 1977), 23.
138 Ibid.
139 E.S. Gerstenberger and W. Schrage, *Suffering*, translated by John E. Steely (Nashville: Abingdon, 1980).
140 Ibid., 103.
141 Ibid.

overcome suffering. Jesus did not engage in interpreting suffering, but demonstrated that suffering could be borne and tran-
scended—in fact, overcome. The vision of the suffering Christ
viewed in the light of the resurrection yields the real meaning
and the real comfort the sufferer needs.

The New Testament offers more than a message of ultimate
healing and comfort—it also challenges the reader to engage in
battling suffering in this earthly life. Therefore, the New Testament discusses suffering in the context of its mastery and conquest. The good news is that no suffering can separate us from
the love of God in Jesus Christ. *The experience of this love,
rather than escape from the pain, is the goal of utmost importance.*

Suffering as Viewed by Augustine

Church history gives us two major views on suffering. The
Augustinian view is based on Genesis 1:31, God saw the created
world and said that it was good. Augustine, Bishop of Hippo in
the early 5th Century, was influenced by Greco-Roman philosophy and Neo-Platonic thought; he identified *being* with *good-
ness*. Suffering, then, is punishment for or due to sin; that is,
suffering results from the human choice to fall into nothingness,
the nothingness out of which God made all things.[142] Suffering is
therefore not necessary, but is inevitable. (God, in his perfect
knowledge, knew that the Fall was inevitable, as human beings
sought to define and create meaning of their lives.)

Suffering as Viewed by Iranæus

Iranæus, Bishop of Lyons in the Second Century, presented
another view of suffering. Even though God creates all and
pronounces it good, he gives people the power to choose to love
him, to grow in likeness to him, although this power of choice
necessarily allowed the possibility of wrong choices: disobedience, hence sin, hence suffering.

---

142 Richard N. Dearing, "Ministry and the Problem of Suffering," *Journal of
Pastoral Care* 39, no. 1 (March 1985), 65.

This view presents the potential for suffering and sin as both necessary and inevitable. Implicit in this view is the suggestion that God takes the risk of culpability in suffering and that this risk is necessary if persons are to elect to love and become like God.[143]

Suffering as Viewed by E. Stanley Jones

A 20th Century statesman who struggled with the question of suffering was E. Stanley Jones, the great missionary to the Hindus. He dealt with this issue in his *Christ and Human Suffering*.[144] Jones saw suffering as a result of evil, and said that there are two kinds of evil. The first evil is sin, which arises from within, from the choices of our will. The second evil comes from without, from our environment of society and natural universe.

Jones lists nine avenues of suffering based on Luke 21:8-19:

1. Sufferings from confused counsels in religion;

2. Suffering from ways and conflicts in human society;

3. Suffering from physical calamities in nature;

4. Suffering from physical sickness and infirmities;

5. Suffering from economic distress;

6. Suffering from acts of one's own fellow men;

7. Suffering from religious and secular authorities;

8. Suffering through the home life; and

9. Suffering from being associated with Christ.

---

143 Ibid.
144 E. Stanley Jones, *Christ and Human Suffering* (New York: Abingdon, 1933).

Universal Responses to Suffering

Jones lists several universal responses to suffering:

1. Remaking the world so that the possibility of suffering is left out (the fantasy of the extremist Persian poet, Omar Khayyam);

2. Accepting the fact of suffering and trying to meet it by always anticipating it;

3. Self-pity;

4. Stoicism;

5. The attitude of Buddha (which finds suffering everywhere);

6. The Hindu concept of Karma and reincarnation;

7. The Muslim acceptance of all suffering as God's will;

8. The Jewish hope based on some Old Testament promises that their nation will be spared; and

9. The basic denial of suffering in Christian Science belief.

Suffering as Viewed by Judaism

Jones comments further on the Jewish response. He says that, to this mentality, the cross does not make sense. God takes care of his people; they will be spared. Jones points out that, although some Christians accept this response, the New Testament does not support this view. Jewish scholar Samuel Karff would disagree with Jones' interpretations of the Jewish attitude. Karff classifies the Jewish response to the question of innocent suffering as follows:

1. Inauthentic righteousness—the innocent may only appear so;

2. The suffering servant—we may suffer for God;

3. The chastisement of love—discipline by God;

4. Reliance on future salvation—the hedge of time;

5. Divine self-limitation—the price of human freedom; and

6. A covenant with a hidden clause—the limitations of human understanding.[145]

Suffering in View of the Cross

A devout follower of Christ, E. Stanley Jones believed that only a solid Christian theology of the cross could adequately deal with the problem of suffering. God, in Jesus, suffered on the cross; God participated in human suffering at the cross, making the darkest hour of history the brightest. The end became the beginning—the cross became the throne!

Jones proclaims: "The Stoic bears, the Epicurean seeks to enjoy, the Buddhist and the Hindu stand apart, disillusioned, the Moslem submits, but only the Christian exults!"[146]

Suffering as Viewed by C.S. Lewis

Several writers offer different highlights of basically similar views. C.S. Lewis, in *The Problem of Pain*, suggests another aspect of pain in his idea that God uses pain as an instrument to call man to submit his will to him. Lewis claims a connection between the function of pain and God's purposes for man:[147]

> We can rest contentedly in our sins and in our stupidities; and anyone who has watched gluttons shoveling down the most exquisite foods as if they did not know what they were eating, will admit that we can ignore even pleasure. But pain insists upon being attended to. God whispers to

---

145 Karff, cited in Shelp and Sunderland, 76-77.
146 Jones, 231.
147 C.S. Lewis, *The Problem of Pain* (New York: Macmillan, 1962), 92-95.

us in our pleasures, speaks in our conscience, but shouts
in our pains: it is his megaphone to rouse a deaf world.[148]

For Lewis, the real problem "is not why some humble, pious,
believing people suffer, but why some do not."[149] Realizing the
controversy of his position, he adds:

> I am not arguing that pain is not painful. Pain hurts. That
> is what the word means. I am only trying to show that the
> old Christian doctrine of being made "perfect through
> suffering" (Heb 2:10) is not incredible.[150]

Suffering as Viewed by Leslie Weatherhead

Another English writer, Leslie Weatherhead, deals with these
same issues in *Why Do Men Suffer*. Weatherhead acknowledges
that the fall of man introduced pain into the world:

> ... Genesis tells us thorns and thistles grew in the Garden
> because man had sinned (Gen 3:18). And Saint Paul cer-
> tainly talks about the whole creation groaning and travail-
> ing in pain waiting for man's redemption ... It may be
> true that germs would never have come into being; that is,
> germs of disease, but for man's sin and folly.[151]

Weatherhead proposes that we trust the wisdom of God, who
designed things in such a way that "a man's safety depends on
his capacity for feeling pain." He summarizes such a Christian
perspective on pain as follows:

1. God cannot prevent pain without altering the whole basis
   of human life and rearranging it on a plan which would be
   far less good than the present one.

2. God is doing everything possible to remove the suffering
   of the innocent in a way consonant with those purposes,

---

148 Ibid., 93.
149 Ibid., 104.
150 Ibid.
151 Leslie D. Weatherhead, *Why Do Men Suffer?* (New York: Abingdon,
     1936), 64.

seen by him from the beginning of time, to be the best for the greatest number.

3. Though he did not send suffering upon the innocent personally, yet the growth of character in those who take the right attitude to pain, the influence such a bearing of pain has on those who watch, is undoubtedly inspired by God.

4. God bears his share of suffering. To rail against the suffering of the innocent is sometimes to forget that one rails against the greatest innocent sufferer. Even the greatest human sufferer can only be silent before the greater suffering of the innocent Lamb of God.

Suffering as Viewed by Dietrich Bonhoeffer

Clearly pain and suffering are intertwined with the problem of evil. Dietrich Bonhoeffer, the Christian theologian who was imprisoned and executed by the Nazis, believed that the question of *why evil exists* is not a useful theological question, for such a question assumes that it is possible to go behind the existence forced upon us as sinners. "If we could answer it then we would not be sinners."[152] "It is not the purpose of the Bible to give information about the origin of evil, but to witness to its character as guilt and as the infinite burden of man," explains Bonhoeffer.[153] "We would be simplifying and completely distorting the biblical narratives if we were simply to involve the devil, who, as God's enemy, caused all this."[154]

The useful theological question, then, does not arise about the origin of evil, but about the real overcoming of evil on the cross. The question asks for the forgiveness of guilt, for the reconciliation of the fallen world.[155] "The fact is that we live between the

---

152 Dietrich Bonhoeffer, *Creation and Fall* (1959; reprint ed., New York: Macmillan, n.d.), 76.
153 Ibid., 65.
154 Ibid., 64.
155 Ibid., 76.

curse and the promise;"[156] both the pleasureful and the painful
are a part of human life.

Suffering as Viewed by George Buttrick

George Buttrick's book, *God, Pain and Evil*, can be very helpful in an investigation of evil and the problem of pain and suffering. Buttrick lists answers that fall short of their goal:

1. Pain is good in itself;

2. Pain has no real existence;

3. Pain comes from our sin in a prior incarnation; and

4. Pain comes from sin, from either our present sin or from
    someone's sin in the past.[157]

Buttrick suggests: "The mystery of pain is always a mystery ....
There are no neat prefabricated answers, but there is an Answer."[158]

Buttrick examines natural evil, historical evil, and personal
evil. "We have to say that God *allows* pain from natural evil. We
cannot say that he inflicts it."[159] God often enters our lives during
times of natural calamity. "Pain turns our eyes from time to the
mystery beyond time. So what we need is not an explanation, but
a salvation."[160] Jesus never minimized historical evil; however,
he knew that historical pains could be redeemed.

Suffering is never objective, says Buttrick. An academic answer to suffering is sure to fail. The problem of suffering finds
its answer as God enters our suffering. His entrance becomes our
door of deliverance. God's suffering is a paradox, a paradox
which can only be understood *in Jesus Christ*. Jesus his Son is

---

156 Ibid., 83.
157 George A. Buttrick, *God, Pain and Evil* (Nashville: Abingdon, 1966), 24-
    37.
158 Ibid., 36-37.
159 Ibid., 45.
160 Ibid., 55.

the "breakthrough"—God's invasion of our history. Suffering begins to make sense in the light of the breakthrough event—the life, death, and resurrection of Jesus. Only those who believe and respond in faith can attain this understanding, as they come to realize that natural evil, historical evil, and personal evil were conquered in this event: "... the event of Christ has changed the bitter waters into a pool of healing."[161]

The alternatives to this perspective, according to Buttrick, are sidestepping the issue, stoicism, and rebellion, all of which leads to spiritual dead ends. The breakthrough, however, does not dispel the mystery of pain, since we do not know all about the snake in the original garden.

Buttrick believes that pain can cause a cleansing from sin and the desire to sin. Pain cleanses from a false worldliness, lovelessness, self-centeredness, and even from the longing for a lost innocence and from subjugation to the dominion of time. Pain can give insights into the meaning of life; pain can give a new understanding of the natural world and human nature, and can even give us a road toward understanding the nature of God.

We will never know just why this earth is destined to experience pain, or why God should employ so strange a servant as the devil, but that ignorance is itself insight: "God's thoughts are not our thoughts, and his ways are not our ways."[162]

The event of the Resurrection of Jesus Christ shows that suffering is transitory, parasitic, and temporary. Buttrick suggests that, since pain and death are events, they cannot be answered either by a formula in science or a theory in philosophy, but only understood in light of another event—the life, death and resurrection of Jesus!

161 Ibid., 125.
162 Ibid., 210.

Suffering as Viewed by Carl Berner

Carl Berner sees suffering in relation to the cross of Jesus Christ. For Berner, suffering can be seen as crosses to be borne by men and women. "Crosses come in many sizes," he says. He lists them in *Why Me, Lord?*:

1. Hereditary crosses;

2. Direct actions of Satan;

3. Biological crosses;

4. Sociological crosses;

5. Self-imposed and psychological crosses;

6. Crosses borne vicariously; and

7. Christian-witness crosses.[163]

Satan is what he is, God is what he is, and we are what we are. This makes cross-bearing unavoidable. There is no life without a cross; neither is there a cross immune to God's power to turn it into a crown.

Suffering as Viewed by Paul Billheimer

Another age-old question, "Why do the righteous suffer?" is examined in *Don't Waste Your Sorrows* by Paul Billheimer. His thesis is that God ordained suffering as on-the-job training for the "Bride-elect" of Christ.[164] Suffering, a consequence of the Fall, is to produce the character, disposition, and compassionate spirit which will be required for rulership in a government where the law of love is supreme.[165] Billheimer argues:

---

163 Carl W. Berner, *Why Me, Lord?* (Minneapolis: Augsburg, 1973), 30-35.
164 Paul E. Billheimer, *Don't Waste Your Sorrows* (Fort Washington, PA: Christian Literature Crusade, 1977), 9.
165 Ibid.

Even after the new birth and the filling with the Holy
Spirit, which are only beginning experiences, greater dimensions of this love are developed only by exercise and
testing. Purity is one thing and maturity is another. The
latter comes through years of suffering.[166]

The infinitely happy God is the supreme sufferer in the
universe ... suffering is inherent in God's universe ...
from all eternity, suffering is inherent in God's economy
... suffering is inherent in a universe that is moral.[167]

Billheimer concludes, "Because tribulation is necessary for the
decentralization of self and the development of deep dimensions
of agape love, the love can be developed only in the school of
suffering."[168]

Suffering as Viewed by Edith Schaeffer

Edith Schaeffer looks at the "reality of battle wounds in the
midst of life" in her book *Affliction*.[169] She exhorts believers not
to cancel out the realities of living on this side of the resurrection
of our bodies.

We are now in the "before"! We must recognize that we
live in an abnormal universe since the Fall, and that the
time of restoration is only coming yet .... The question—
Why?—is without an answer for our finite minds, except
in the concept of the total picture of what history has been
since the Fall.[170]

Persecution and affliction are a normal part of the Christian
life; all Christians must deal with affliction. We don't know why
each individual accident and death has taken place, but we know
that though there is a fierce battle with heavy casualties, the

---

166 Ibid., 10-11.
167 Ibid., 29-32.
168 Ibid., 10.
169 Edith Schaeffer, *Affliction* (Old Tappan: Revell, 1978), 26.
170 Ibid.

victory is sure and absolute![171] God shares our affliction. In our own struggles, we are not alone in history.

The criterion of the presence of God in us is "not an unbroken flow of answered requests."[172] Schaeffer exhorts us to see the bigger picture. We must watch our priorities. Our bodies are important and will be raised from the dead, but our bodies are not at the moment more important than our inward and spiritual growth as growing personalities, children born into God's family.[173] We must see and feel, and know in our hearts and minds, that we really have a treasure in our weak selves, a light that is not to be hidden within these earthen vessels. This perspective will enable us to endure to the end.

Schaeffer believes that all Christians are to go through a refining process. We are God's workmanship; we are part of something really big. We can imagine ourselves as musicians needing constant practice, or as instruments needing mellowing and refining through years of being made and used. Our *today* has a reality of meaning beyond the present.[174] Thus we can pray, "Thank You that, while I cannot understand everything, my hand is held by the eternal, all-wise, Infinite God, the Creator."[175]

Suffering as Viewed by Paul Tournier

Paul Tournier deals with the issue of suffering and its relationship to creativity in *Creative Suffering*. He says that there is a relationship between the misfortunes which befall mankind, both in the lives of individuals and in those of nations, and the benefits that they enjoy, their progress, and their creativity.[176] However, "the question it raises is a difficult and complex one, and especially dangerous and repellent if it suggests that the relation-

---

171 Ibid., 28-29.
172 Ibid., 39.
173 Ibid., 124.
174 Ibid., 168.
175 Ibid., 210.
176 Paul Tournier, *Creative Suffering* (San Francisco: Harper and Row, 1981), 20.

ship is one of cause and effect, or that suffering has didactic value."[177]

The fact is, evil is everywhere mixed with good, yet in the mixture there is no confusion. Good is the cause of good, and evil causes evil.

Evil cannot be the cause of good. Good cannot be the cause of evil. The relationship between suffering and creativity is that of "succession, not of cause." Tragic events become occasions for victories of good over evil through the way we react to them.

> I am convinced that God wills not death, but life; not disease, but healing. God has *called us* simply because in this fallen world there is disease, suffering, and death, and because the important thing is the way men and women face up to this brutal reality.[178]

Tournier points to Buddha's answer to suffering, which he found "in disinterested love, in renunciation, in the willing acceptance of deprivation." Refusing to react to evil is not the right solution to the problem; what we need to do is to face the suffering issue courageously. Tournier believes that God uses evil for our salvation: "That is what happened on the cross, where the most unjust evil turns out to be the greatest blessing."[179] Christian hope inspires the sufferer because such hope "is not a thing, but a person."[180]

---

177 Ibid.
178 Ibid., 69.
179 Ibid., 119.
180 Ibid., 140.

Suffering as Viewed by Carl Glover

In *Victorious Suffering*, Carl Glover traces three sources of suffering:

1. Law;

2. Human relationships; and

3. Human free will.[181]

Glover also lists several inappropriate and unhealthy human responses to suffering:

1. Resentment;

2. Self-pity;

3. Stoicism;

4. Denial of the reality of suffering;

5. Substituted excitements; and

6. Meek resignation.

Jesus' willing submission was not a weak resignation to suffering, but a *purposeful* acceptance of it. The Christian attitude, following his example, immobilizes suffering and limits the scope of its hurtfulness. Furthermore, the Christian attitude "actually transforms the experience into a means of personal enrichment." The Christian faith provides a climate in which "many questions about the meaning of suffering are satisfactorily answered, and the questions that are not answered fall into their positions of relative unimportance."[182]

---

181 Carl A. Glover, *Victorious Suffering* (New York: Abingdon-Cokesbury, n.d.), 13-26.
182 Ibid., 155-156.

Suffering as Viewed by Ruth Vaughn

How can any approach to suffering bring about a meaningful and healing experience for the one who is actually suffering? How does purposeful acceptance transform our experience of suffering so much that it limits its scope? I was encouraged when I came across one sufferer, Ruth Vaughn, who experienced the meaning of personal suffering and recorded her experiences. Her insights are documented in her book, *My God! My God! Answers to Our Anguished Cries.*[183]

A highly motivated self-achiever, Vaughn never expected to slow down. To her great dismay, her active life came to a sudden halt with a debilitating and painful terminal disease. This highly educated professional woman, whose life had been "like a magical-musical carousel," was forced to deal with suffering. Her screaming start in this direction taught her some rich lessons.

Although she did not find an answer to the question "Why?," Vaughn was able to glimpse a great deal of meaning for her own life and learned some wonderful lessons about life as a Christian believer engaged in suffering. She was able to give up her simplistic theological equations and grasp the meaning of the presence of her Redeemer God, based on Psalm 91:1.

Vaughn had to deal with the fact that she prayed for a miracle and nothing external happened. She demanded "explanation, justification, miracle;" all she found was a vast silence. Her Christian friends remained unwilling to deal with the truth of her situation. As she struggled (mostly alone), she "experienced no divine revelations, theological explanations, surprising inspirations, or dramatic miracles ... and yet ... the inner seething had calmed."[184]

Vaughn learned from personal experience with God that, although the old Puritan truism that "suffering teaches" is too

---

183 Ruth Vaughn, *My God! My God! Answers to Our Anguished Cries* (Nashville: Impact, 1982), 106.
184 Ibid., 70.

simplistic to be a truth, when deep pain is endured with an openness of spirit, one does learn vital clues that aid in comprehending suffering. This assists in putting one's suffering into an understandable perspective that makes its ravages bearable— even, in a certain sense, filled with wonder.[185] Vaughn discovered that God is our Redeemer of circumstances as well as our Redeemer of sins.

> God does not punish by illness or broken life-plans ... If He does, Jesus Christ did not reveal him rightly ... God does not cause either pain or joy. God works in and through the tragedies and happinesses of the haphazard of earthly life, making redemptive use of everything.[186]

Vaughn concluded that God created her not to *do*, but to *be*. The best answer for grief and sorrow "does not come in words. It comes in the God-man who journeyed human tragedy before us."[187] In the absence of external miracles, Vaughn:

> ... learned to walk in the blackness with Him, helpless, dependent, aware of [my] need of Him ... knowing that, in that unpleasant groping journey, I would learn lessons which would escape me in the busyness and fulfillment of light ... He would not deliver me from the brokenness of my world. He would use the brokenness in his way, in His time.[188]

With her new insights, Vaughn built a new world for herself upon the following resolutions:

1. I believe in my personal worth.

2. I will understand and accept my body.

3. When I am weak or tired, I will not think.

4. I will refuse self-recrimination.

---

185 Ibid., 78.
186 Ibid., 89.
187 Ibid., 123.
188 Ibid., 133.

5. I will refuse envy.

6. I will refuse the word, "why"!

7. I will be a compassionate, caring adult-friend to my terrified child-self.

8. I will rejoice in the person I am becoming ... because of God's redemption.

9. Life is going to go on.

10. God is with me.   *He is in my future*

11. Death is only a door to the longer life.

Jesus accepted human existence unequivocally, says Vaughn.

> He accepted evil and suffering as part of this world ... He did not ask who was to blame. He did not ask why it was fact ... No explanation of suffering in the Gospels ... The more I study Jesus, the more I believe that the way that has so plagued my soul is irrelevant.[189]

As Vaughn learned that suffering is something basic and integral to human life, like sharps and flats are to music, she began to let her Redeemer God enable her to make creative use of her old-world debris—to build a new world. She was thus able to transform her *why* into *worship*.

---

189 Ibid., 165.

Suffering as Viewed by Thomson K. Mathew

Vaughn confirms for me the real possibility of developing a positive and constructive personal attitude in the midst of suffering. No one seems to suffer more than a person in excruciating physical pain. Even in cancer patients, the suffering is utmost when there is physical pain involved. Vaughn demonstrates that even in very difficult situations, a Christ-centered attitude is not only possible but practical. This understanding has helped me immensely in my pastoral care ministry.

As terrible as suffering is, I believe that it can be an arena in which human personality can grow. I have seen many persons growing in their personalities as they have dealt positively with their suffering, even as they continued to trust God for their healing. Every sufferer potentially stands to grow in his personality if he can properly deal with his suffering. The temptation for the sufferer, however, is to "perceive the possibilities or realities of suffering only as destructive and withdraw into an inner fantasy asylum or dumb existence."[190] This can only lead people to despair and anxiety. On the other hand, if the sufferer faces the experience courageously, he can expect to make some of the most vital discoveries of his life. I was pleased to see this notion supported in D.A. Carson's recent *Reflections on Suffering and Evil: How Long, O Lord?*, which biblically and pastorally examines the problem of evil from an evangelical perspective.[191]

Let me attempt to summarize and synthesize this inquiry. The Bible does not offer all the details about the origin of evil. This remains a mystery beyond human comprehension. We cannot fully understand this mystery because we are fallen people, sinners who have fallen and are falling. The fact is that evil exists alongside good in this world.

---

190 Dearing, 62-63.
191 D.A. Carson, *Reflections on Suffering and Evil: How Long, O Lord?* (Grand Rapids: Baker, 1990).

Christians are not exempt from all the laws of nature or the forces of evil during their lifetimes in this present world. Satan is involved in evil, but his involvement is more than a simplistic cause-and-effect matter.

Jesus did not explain evil, although he acknowledged its presence, confronted it with boldness and authority in his ministry, and overcame it on the cross. Evil has been defeated, and Christ is alive to sustain that victory in our present time.

We have the privilege of praying for deliverance from evil. God does answer our prayers, but he does not always answer the way we want. While I believe and have witnessed miraculous physical healing, I agree with E. Stanley Jones that "God should not be reduced to a great wiper of tears." Real comfort often comes as a byproduct of inner spiritual victories. God does not inflict suffering, but suffering is not purposeless, nor is it meaningless. God redeems our suffering when we live our lives in the light of the cross.

Mortal life must be viewed in the context of eternal life. Only the cross and the resurrection give true meaning to human suffering. Someday there will no longer be any suffering; only then will we understand fully the mystery of evil and suffering. By then, we will be fully redeemed and the groaning of the whole creation will have ceased (Rom 8:18, 22).

Becoming settled about the question of suffering is important for the pastoral caregiver, because the theological question of suffering often comes up in pastoral conversations. The minister who has not settled the issue personally will find himself getting anxious and defensive. Jesus has not called us to be his defense lawyers; he has called us to be his witnesses.

My experience with suffering individuals is that *their need to ask "why"* is more important than their need to get an answer. Most of the questioners seem to know that we do not know the answers to their unanswerable questions. They seem to accept it well; still they have a need to raise the questions. Our giving them permission to ask the questions without becoming anxious or defensive is in itself a healing treatment. Job's friends were not very good caregivers. (They have followers of this age who are not much better.) Let the sufferer ask the *why?* question without feeling guilt. Offer any comfort, if you can, based on your own theology of suffering. Keep in mind that simplistic answers do not satisfy the sufferers and may cause them to lose their respect for you. It is better to freely admit when you don't know the answer. If you can tolerate the *why?* question well, you might eventually be trusted to help a sufferer to move from the *why* question to the more important *what* question: "What is it that the Lord wants me to do now?"

8

A Spirit-Led Model for Pastoral Care

Introduction

As the pastoral care movement in America reached a comfortable level of maturity in regard to theology and practice, the American Pentecostal movement was still in its adolescence. Because of its holiness and revivalist orientation, the Pentecostal movement was concerned with salvation of souls far more than the care of souls. Although pastoral care was occurring in a large segment of American churches, Pentecostal pastoral care appears to have been more evangelistic than pastoral in nature. When one considers the fact that the pastoral care movement itself was a "liberal" reaction against the traditional denominational ministry, the ultra-conservative perspective of the Pentecostals regarding pastoral care becomes understandable. As a result of the emphasis on the salvation rather than the care of souls, few written materials regarding early Pentecostal perspectives of pastoral care exist. This seeming neglect of the care of souls cannot be viewed, however, as a fault of the Pentecostal movement itself. It is a phenomenon to be understood from an historical perspective.[192]

Historical Perspective

There are three dynamic characteristics of early 20th Century Pentecostalism that contributed to the neglect of comprehensive relational pastoral care.

Charismatic Worship

Pentecostals have always been charismatic worshippers, expecting the gifts of the Spirit to be manifested in the worship service. The needs of people were often met through the work of the Holy Spirit in the service. The pastor, as shepherd of the flock, functioned as the administrator of divine healing. He was expected to pray for healing, and especially for miracles. Although anointing with oil often accompanied these prayers, the emphasis was on the divine act, not on human touch or relationship.

Puritanical Holiness

The puritanical holiness to which the Pentecostals were committed also affected the practice of pastoral care. From such an ethical perspective, troubled persons were sinners to be dealt with, rather than candidates for caregiving. This was not unique to Pentecostals, but they saw themselves as people called by God to holiness and separation from the world. This meant separation from divorce, alcoholism and other sins, and from those who participated in them. Disciplinary actions were often initiated against people who took part in such sins. As a result, there was neither theology nor felt need to develop pastoral approaches to these worldly problems.

---

192 An earlier version of this chapter was published in John Vining and Edward Decker, eds., *Soul Care: A Pentecostal/Charismatic Perspective* (Rockaway, NY: Cummings and Hathaway, 1996).

Eschatological Evangelism

A third characteristic affecting the practice of Pentecostal pastoral care was the eschatological evangelism to which Pentecostals were committed. Eschatological evangelism approached everyone, in all situations, with one question: "If you die today, would you go to heaven?" Rooted in a deep commitment to win the lost for Christ, this approach was more propositional than relational. Consequently, opportunities for support and expressions of care, such as a funeral service, were seen as opportunities for evangelistic crusade. The almost inevitable altar call eclipsed any potential development of relational approaches to pastoral practice.

Because of this history, identifying a clinical model of pastoral care remains unimportant to a great number of Pentecostals and charismatics even today; still no definitive Pentecostal theology of pastoral care exists. For this reason many Pentecostals and charismatics who venture into clinical pastoral education report that clinical training is a wilderness experience for them. They have no biblical or theological rationale for the experiences they encounter and in which they find themselves involved.

Compatibility with Biblical Theology

In spite of the theological challenges of the training experience, many Pentecostals and charismatics who press on to complete Clinical Pastoral Education discover that several foundational tenets of a comprehensive model of pastoral care are compatible with Pentecostal biblical theology. For instance, Boisen's concept of the living human document[193] is a Pauline concept (2 Cor 3:2). Nouwen's concept of the wounded healer,[194] in spite of its Catholic origin and image of powerlessness, is acceptable to Pentecostals who are committed to divine healing.

---

193 Gerkin, *The Living Human Document.*
194 Nouwen, *The Wounded Healer.*

Rogers' concept of unconditional positive regard[195] has much in common with the biblical fruit of the Spirit.

Biblical Counseling Concepts

Counseling concepts such as empathy, concreteness, immediacy, warmth, active listening and hospitality can be seen as non-traditional expressions of biblical concepts. All of these, when properly understood, are compatible with Pentecostal theology. Thus, the historical lack of Pentecostal and charismatic interest in clinical pastoral care is due to the characteristics mentioned above, not to a theology that would limit pastoral activities to the altar ministry.

Therefore, a comprehensive model of pastoral care can be described which is distinctly Pentecostal. This model retains the passionate commitment to historic teachings regarding the gifts and present operations of the Holy Spirit, while enhancing the Spirit-led minister's ability to make himself available to the Holy Spirit for ministry to the people of God in their daily lives as well as in worship services. Such a perspective is able to balance the disjunction of the occurrence of miracles as well as the lack of them. It infuses the truth of God's Word into the realities of actual life situations in which persons find themselves. A pastoral care perspective is useful in institutional settings as well as in the local church, but it must be based on biblical evidence, clinical experience, and theological reflection.

A Distinctly Pentecostal Model

Such a model first appears in the Gospels, which contain stories about the daily ministry of Jesus as well as about his miracles. From these accounts it is evident that much more than impartation of miracles occurred in his ministry. Jesus met the needs of people not only with the miraculous, but also with the ongoing daily care of his presence. The Good Shepherd provided pastoral care. Jesus ministered between the miracles.

---

195 Carl Rogers, *On Becoming a Person* (Boston: Houghton, 1961).

Upon close examination, the gospel of John provides detailed descriptions of Christ's ministry between the miracles. For example, the sixth chapter of John begins with two great miracles: Jesus fed the five thousand, then calmed the sea. The rest of chapter six and the next two chapters contain no miracles; then chapter nine begins again with miracles. What may be discerned from this overview of Scripture is that Jesus' ministry between the miracles contained four distinct activities:

1. He enabled people to hear the voice of God,

2. He enabled people to learn the will of God,

3. He enabled people to live Kingdom life, and

4. He enabled people to live a life of loyalty to the Father.

Enabling Persons to Listen to the Voice of God

The feeding of five thousand in the gospel of John is followed by a lengthy discourse on the bread of life (Jn 6:25-59), the central focus of which is "Attend to God! Listen to Him!" This record of Jesus' words is presented between the miracles of chapters six and nine. This placement is more than mere coincidence. It teaches us that the good news of the gospel contains much to be heard, even when no miracle is occurring.

Like the hungry multitude, *persons in need of care often find it difficult to focus on anything other than their need*. Well-meaning friends and family frequently offer suggestions as to how to alleviate the felt need; the myriad of voices often becomes confusing. What is needed at crisis times is for persons in need of care to hear one voice clearly. It is the responsibility and privilege of the Spirit-led caregiver to enable those who need ministry to clearly hear the voice of God. It is important to enable others to hear the voice of God within and to hear God speaking through the circumstances they encounter.

Only a person engaged in keen listening can enable another to hear God. Henri Nouwen pointed this out in *The Wounded Healer* by suggesting that ministry involves the articulation of inner events. God does speak through the Holy Spirit, but only those whose ears are attuned to him will hear his voice (Rev 2:7). Enabling individuals to hear the voice of God within, and make sense of what they are hearing, is a goal of Spirit-led pastoral care. It is the responsibility of the Spirit-led caregiver to enable those to whom he or she ministers to hear the voice of the Spirit, who is already in dialogue with them.

Spirit-led pastoral care is based on a definition of ministry which sees ministry as being in dialogue with the world, while at the same time being in dialogue with God. In this regard, the Spirit-led model of pastoral care is in harmony with various counseling theories, especially client-centered therapy. This theory provides the caregiver with useful concepts such as empathy, warmth, unconditional positive regard, congruence, concreteness, immediacy, and active listening. Rogers,[196] Carkhuff,[197] and others have defined these terms and established their usefulness.

The distinctive difference in Spirit-led pastoral care is that both the counselor and the client engage in listening, especially to the inner voice of the Spirit. By enabling the client to listen to the voice of the Spirit and by articulating the inner events as needed, the Spirit-led caregiver ministers to the client. As C.S. Lewis suggested, God whispers to us in our pleasures, speaks to us in our consciences, and shouts to us in our pains.[198]

This focus on listening and hearing also leaves the door open for the manifestations of the charismata. For instance, words of wisdom and words of knowledge can be a part of the listening/hearing process of caregiving. This makes it a distinctively Pentecostal ministry.

---

196 Ibid.
197 Roberts R. Carkhuff, *The Art of Helping* (Scotsdale, PA: Herald Press, 1972).
198 C.S. Lewis, *The Problem of Pain*.

Enabling Persons to Learn the Will of God

Another observation from the Gospel of John is that ministry between miracles can be seen as teaching. Reading the discourse on the bread of life, it becomes evident that the feeding of five thousand was more than just for the purpose of meeting the physical needs of those in attendance. The purpose of the feeding was also didactic in nature: it was a teaching/learning event. It was intended to enable those in attendance to learn the will of God, and it did so by reference to what they already knew and to what they had just experienced.

Teaching the Word of God has always been a matter of primary importance to Pentecostals and charismatics. Spirit-led pastors are regularly engaged in preaching and Bible teaching.

Appropriate teaching of the Word is an integral part of Spirit-led pastoral care. Unfortunately, Pentecostal pastoral care has traditionally included frequent use of a shortcut technique called "proof texting," which is the practice of using biblical texts pulled out of context to try to offer comfort or encouragement, or to establish theological positions.

The fields of counseling and education give us examples of teaching as an effective part of caregiving. For example, the re-education of clients is an important aspect of cognitive approaches to therapy and of rational emotive therapy. In the field of education, educating the "whole person" has become an important issue. Education is now seen as a lifelong process of growth and development. Malcolm Knowles[199] believes that adults as students must be seen as people of experience. What is taught must connect with the adult's self-concept and life experience. He also believes that adult learners want the teaching they receive to address the various problems of their lives.

This andragogical approach to enabling people to learn the Word and will of God presents a good model of caregiving ministry for the Pentecostal and charismatic. The Word of God

---

199 Malcolm C. Knowles, *The Modern Practice of Adult Education.*

can be taught in light of people's self-concept, experience, problems, and need for application. The purpose of Spirit-led pastoral care, however, is more than information-sharing. This model allows the caregiver to move the client from simply gathering information to the integration of information. The client is then able to apply the Word of God to his/her life situation.

Jesus offers excellent examples of this type of caregiving. With his keen understanding of people and their experiences, he directly addressed their problems and issues. He offered them opportunities for practical application of the principles he taught. This is the method of teaching he modeled for his disciples; Jesus enables his followers to learn of him (Mt 11:29).

Seeing pastoral care as a ministry of teaching the Word of God opens up various avenues of caregiving for Pentecostals and charismatics. From this perspective, preaching and Christian education are pastoral care ministries. This view also moves pastoral care beyond the professional area of ordained ministry and opens the door for various forms of lay caregiving ministries.

Enabling Persons to Live the Kingdom Life

One temptation faced by people who believe in miracles is that they desire to postpone living until the miracle occurs. This is not biblical. Waiting, praying, and anticipating a miracle also includes continuing to live at the fullest potential possible. Spirit-led approaches to soul care enable persons to do just that: to live the kingdom life.

Between the miracles recorded in John 6 and 9, Jesus lived the kingdom life. He walked throughout Galilee. He taught in the synagogue. He engaged in dialogue with family, friends and foes. He ministered to the condemned and frightened. He rested and he ate. He was fully alive every day, ministering between miracles by his presence, concern and teaching.

Life for Jesus meant being in relationship with God and the world. It included sacred and mundane activities. He went to the temple. He visited people. He attended weddings. He blessed children. In his ministry, Jesus never proposed any escape from reality. The joy that he knew was set before him enabled him to not only endure the cross but also to overcome it.

Enabling persons to live between the miracles is traditionally known as *guiding* and *sustaining*.[200] *Guiding* is that activity that directs persons in appropriate ways of living. It reminds them of the truth. *Sustaining* is that activity that provides support through difficult times. These care ministries enable Spirit-led caregivers to lead and sustain others through the tumult of life, in full knowledge that the crisis will end. The activities of guiding and sustaining enable people to live, move, and have their being in Christ. Rather than going from miracle worker to miracle worker, persons learn to walk with the source of the miracles— Jesus Christ.

Spirit-led pastoral care must include walking with people through the valleys of life. Guiding and sustaining the bereaved or the battered, the Spirit-led caregiver can lead them through the grief process or crisis intervention, knowing that the light of the resurrection is always ahead of them. The miracle of Easter must be an ever-present reality to the Spirit-filled caregiver.

This is a ministry of incarnational presence. Pastoral care-giving should be modeled after Jesus' walk with the disciples who went to Emmaus. He walked with them and talked with them, and ultimately revealed the reality of the resurrection to them. Jesus listened to these confused disciples. He articulated their inner events in such a way that they themselves could listen, hear and even verbalize what was inside them. He also enabled them to learn to apply the Word of the Lord, by asking them what Moses and the prophets had to say about the issue at hand (Lk 24:27). He guided them to their destination and ulti-mately broke bread with them in fellowship. In this process, which culminated in the deepest form of *koinonia*, they were able to receive a new perspective and begin a new journey of faith.

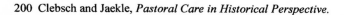

200 Clebsch and Jaekle, *Pastoral Care in Historical Perspective.*

Enabling Persons to Live a Life of Loyalty to Jesus

The final component of a Pentecostal/charismatic perspective of pastoral care is that people need to learn to live a life of loyalty to Jesus. In the sixth chapter of John, there are two miracles, followed by a mass exodus of what was at one time a group of eager followers. Jesus then asked his disciples a poignant question; Jesus asked them if they, too, wanted to depart (Jn 6:67). Peter responded: "Lord, to whom shall we go? You have the words of eternal life" (Jn 6:68).

This vignette demonstrates a basic principle: *When the miracles delay, people need to stay.* People need to stay steady, stay loyal, stay with Jesus. Spirit-led pastoral care is ministry that enables people to stay loyal to Jesus Christ during these dark and cloudy periods of life, when it is easy to forget that eternal life is more important than relief from external circumstances. The Spirit-led pastoral caregiver can remind people that only Jesus has the words of eternal life. Between miracles, one must hold on to him and remain loyal to him. He is still there with us, ministering to us between the miracles.

Assumptions

Several assumptions are foundational to this perspective of soul care:

God at Work

First, God is at work in his world. Scripture says the earth is the Lord's, and the fullness thereof (Ps. 24:1). While faith is an important component of miracles, some miracles happen as the result of the patients' faith (Lk 7:9), and others happen because of the faith of the community of faith (Mk 2:5). For example, the resurrection of Lazarus could hardly have been the result of his own faith (Jn 11:39). The community of faith, not the patient alone, carries the burden of faith. Still other miracles occur at God's behest and come as a surprise. He is at work daily, ministering life and healing.

A Model Built on Hope

Second, this model is built on hope. There is hope in the person of Jesus Christ. As long as he lives, the hope for divine intervention exists. While it is recognized that some chapters of our lives contain no miracles, other chapters containing miracles are yet to come. Because God is at work in the world, hope is possible. Because hope is available, people can remain loyal to Christ.

The Kingdom and the Power

This model assumes that the Kingdom of God came when Jesus did (Mt 12:28) and that the kingdom is in the midst of us now through the presence and power of Jesus who sent us the Holy Spirit (Lk 17:21). The Holy Spirit is at work in our midst here and now. There is a full dimension of the Kingdom that is yet to come (Mt 6:10). We look to its dawn as we seek the coming of our Lord (Mt 6:10). This leaves the possibility of ultimate healing for all God's people.

God's Time

God's time is not our timeline. Clinical realities and other realities of life manifest in chronological time, but miracles occur in God's time. The Bible indicates that some things happen only in the fullness of time. For instance, as far as Joseph and Mary were concerned, the birth of Jesus took place on the human timeline (*chronos*), but the coming of the kingdom occurred in God's fullness of time (*kairos*).

While one anticipates the *kairos*, one lives in the clinical realities of *chronos*; yet because the eternal God intervenes in our time, we have *kairos* moments. While we await eventual eternity with the "I AM," we can worship God, listen to him, learn of him, live for him, and be loyal to him in the *chronos* (on our human timeline).

Wholeness as Healing

This caregiving model assumes that God heals in many ways. Sometimes he heals instantly, sometimes gradually. One form of healing is not necessarily better than the other, as God's purpose may be something greater than the immediate relief we desire. Healing of the mind and the spirit are at least as important as healing of the body. God alone is ultimately the healer of us all. His will is our well being as whole persons. In this sense, God's will is our wholeness.

Since healing is wholeness, not just physical healing, and God's will always is that we become the whole persons he created us to be, then there is no need to begin our prayers for healing with "If it be Your will." It is always God's will to heal, although sometimes we will see a healing of the body and other times it will be a healing of the mind and spirit.

Summary

In summary, this Spirit-led model of pastoral care is built on biblical and theological assumptions such as a theology of hope and the reality of God at work in the world. It postulates that caregiving is an active process of listening, learning, living, and remaining loyal in spite of circumstances. It rests upon a series of assumptions, the sum of which is that God cares, and is concerned about complete healing, and will heal—in his perfect timing.

Goals and Methods of Spirit-Led Soul Care

The ultimate goal of Spirit-led pastoral care is the wholeness of those receiving care. Wholeness involves an acceptance of self and of the situations encountered. It is the active pursuit of healthy living, be it physical, emotional, or spiritual. People are made whole when they can hear the voice of God, learn to understand his Word, accept his will within their specific contexts, live by faith daily, and remain committed to Christ regardless of the circumstances of life.

No specific methods or techniques accomplish this. Rather, this model of pastoral care emphasizes the personal qualities of the caregiver, such as empathy, warmth, and other interpersonal assets. This model allows the discriminating use of appropriate methods of counseling. There is room for active listening, responding, "carefronting," and other methods that will enable the care-receiver to listen to the inner voice of the Spirit. Andragogical/pedagogical skills are important to enable the client to learn. Cognitive, reality, and behavioral techniques can be utilized to challenge the care-receiver to live a fully human life. Skills in discipling and spiritual direction are needed to help the care-receiver grow in grace and live a life of loyalty to Christ.

Traditionally, caregivers have been referred to as healers, guides, sustainers, and reconcilers.[201] They have been described as listeners, understanders and comforters;[202] teachers, preachers, counselors, organizers, and celebrators;[203] monitors of the community of faith, maintainers of the community, strengtheners of the community, and facilitators of *koinonia* (fellowship), *eucharista* (celebration),and *diakonia* (service).[204]

From a Pentecostal/charismatic perspective, however, the caregiver is one who enables faith and who comforts in times of need. Thus, rather than relying solely on training, skills, or human qualities (although all are important), Spirit-led caregivers rely on God. God is the ultimate source of healing (Jn 14:16), and it is he who empowers the caregiver, through the Holy Spirit. Not only does the Holy Spirit empower his ministers for this service, but he also leads and directs the caregiving situation. Trusting that God knows what is needed and is guiding the care, Spirit-led caregivers are able to be real persons; they can offer to others the comfort they have received from God (2 Cor 1:3-4).

---

201 Clebsch and Jaekle, 4.
202 Oden, *Pastoral Theology*, 156.
203 Henri Nouwen, *Creative Ministry*.
204 Shelp and Sunderland, *A Biblical Basis for Ministry*.

Those receiving care are not just patients or parishioners. By faith, they become children of God, inheritors of the kingdom of God. Consequently, persons in need of pastoral care are brothers and sisters in need: broken and battered perhaps, but with the capacity to listen, learn, live, and be loyal to God; capable, but in need of enabling. Even unbelievers are seen as family members in this model, for they too can be encouraged to hear the prompting of the Spirit, which calls all people to repentance. Thus, Spirit-led soul care embraces evangelism as an act of love rather than a crusade or conquest.

Conclusion

This chapter presented a model of pastoral care that views caregiving as ministry between miracles. This ministry enables persons to:

1. Listen to the voice of God,

2. Learn the will of God,

3. Live fully human lives, and

4. Remain loyal to Jesus Christ.

This uniquely Spirit-led model of soul care represents an integration of various counseling, psychological, and educational principles, as well as biblical and theological insights. Finally, it rests upon a series of assumptions, including a theology of hope and the reality that God is at work in his world. God cares, and he will bring comfort, reconciliation, restoration, and healing.

Works Cited

Berenson, B., and R. Carkhuff, eds. *Sources of Gain in Counseling and Psychotherapy.* New York: Holt, Rinehart and Winston, 1967.

Berner, Carl W. *Why Me, Lord?* Minneapolis: Augsburg, 1973.

Billheimer, Paul E. *Don't Waste Your Sorrows.* Fort Washington, PA: Christian Literature Crusade, 1977.

Bonhoeffer, Dietrich. *Creation and Fall.* 1959: Reprint ed. New York: Macmillan, n.d.

Brister, C.W. *Pastoral Care in the Church.* New York: Harper and Row, 1964.

Buttrick, George A. *God, Pain and Evil.* Nashville: Abingdon, 1966.

Caregiver Journal 2, no. 1.

Carkhuff, Robert R. *The Art of Helping.* Scottsdale, PA: Herald Press, 1972.

_____. *Beyond Counseling and Therapy.* New York: Holt, Rinehart and Winston, 1977.

Carson, D.A. *Reflections on Suffering and Evil: How Long, O Lord?* Grand Rapids: Baker, 1990.

Clebsch, William A. and Charles R. Jaekle, eds. *Pastoral Care in Historical Perspective.* Englewood Cliffs, NJ: Prentice-Hall, 1964.

Clinebell, Howard J. *Basic Types of Pastoral Counseling.* Nashville: Abingdon, 1966.

_____. *Contemporary Growth Therapies.* Nashville: Abingdon, 1981.

Corey, Gerald. *Theory and Practice of Counseling and Psychotherapy.* 2nd ed. Monterey, CA: Brooks/Cole, 1982.

Dearing, Richard N. "Ministry and the Problem of Suffering." *Journal of Pastoral Care* 39, no. 1 (March 1985).

Erikson, Erik H. *Childhood and Society.* 2nd ed. New York: W.W. Norton, 1964.

Egan, Gerard. *The Skilled Helper.* Monterey, CA: Brooks/Cole, 1982.

Fowler, James W. *Stages of Faith.* San Francisco: Harper and Row, 1981.

Gerkin, Charles V. *The Living Human Document: Revisioning Pastoral Counseling in a Hermeneutical Mode.* Nashville: Abingdon, 1984.

Gerstenberger, E.S. and W. Schrage. *Suffering.* Translated by John W. Steely. Nashville: Abingdon, 1980.

Glover, Carl A. *Victorious Suffering.* New York: Abingdon-Cokesbury, n.d.

Havighurst, Robert J. *Developmental Tasks and Education.* New York: David Makay Company, 1961.

Hiltner, Seward. *Preface to Pastoral Counseling.* Nashville: Abingdon, 1958.

Hoekendijk, J.C. *The Church Inside Out.* Philadelphia: Westminster, 1966.

Holifield, E. Brooks. *A History of Pastoral Care in America.* Nashville: Abingdon, 1983.

Hulme, William. *Pastoral Care and Counseling.* Minneapolis, Augsburg, 1981.

Hyatt, Eddie, Jr. *2000 Years of Charismatic Christianity.* Tulsa: Hyatt International Ministries, 1996.

Ivy, Steven S. "Pastoral Diagnosis is Pastoral Caring." *Journal of Pastoral Care* 42, no. 1 (spring 1988).

Jackson, Edgar N. *Understanding Grief.* New York: Abingdon, 1957.

_____. *When Someone Dies.* Philadelphia: Fortress, 1973.

Jones, E. Stanley. *Christ and Human Suffering.* New York: Abingdon, 1933.

Knowles, Malcolm S. *The Modern Practice of Adult Education.* New York: Cambridge/The Adult Education Company, 1980.

_____. *The Modern Practice of Adult Education.* New York: Associated Press, 1980.

Lester, Andrew D. *Hope in Pastoral Care and Counseling.* Louisville: Westminster, 1995.

Lewis, C.S. *The Problem of Pain.* New York: Macmillan, 1962.

Mayeroff, M. *On Caring.* New York: Harper and Row, 1971.

Mead, Sydney E. "The Rise of the Evangelical Conception of the Ministry in America: 1607-1850." In *The Ministry in Historical Perspectives,* edited by H. Richard Niebuhr and Daniel D. Williams. San Francisco: Harper and Row, 1983.

Messer, Donald E. *Contemporary Images of Christian Ministry.* Nashville: Abingdon, 1989.

Michaelsen, Robert S. "Protestant Ministry in America: 1850-1950." In *The Ministry in Historical Perspectives,* edited by H. Richard Niebuhr and Daniel D. Williams. San Francisco: Harper and Row, 1983.

Miller, William R. and Kathleen A. Jackson. *Practical Psychology for Pastors.* Englewood Cliffs, NJ: Prentice-Hall, 1985.

Niebuhr, H. Richard. *The Purpose of the Church and Its Ministry.* New York: Harper, 1956.

Niebuhr, H. Richard and Daniel D. Williams, eds. *The Ministry in Historical Perspectives.* San Francisco: Harper and Row, 1983.

Nouwen, Henry J.M. *Creative Ministry.* Garden City: Image, 1971.

_____. *In the Name of Jesus.* New York: Crossroad, 1989.

_____. *The Wounded Healer.* Garden City, NY: Doubleday, 1972.

Oden, Thomas C. *Classical Pastoral Care.* 4 vols. Grand Rapids: Baker Books, 1987-94.

_____. *Kerygma and Counseling.* Philadelphia: Westminster, 1966.

_____. *Pastoral Theology: Essentials of Ministry.* San Francisco: Harper and Row, 1983.

Pruyser, Paul W. *The Minister as Diagnostician.* Philadelphia: Westminster Press, 1978.

Rogers, Carl. *On Becoming a Person.* Boston: Houghton, 1961.

_____. "The Conditions of Change from a Client-Centered Viewpoint." In *Sources of Gain in Counseling and Psychotherapy,* edited by B. Berenson and R. Carkhuff. New York: Holt, Rinehart and Winston, 1967.

Salsbery, William D. "Equipping and Mobilizing Believers to Perform a Shared Ministry of Pastoral Care." D.Min. Dissertation, Oral Roberts University, 1991.

Schaeffer, Edith. *Affliction.* Old Tappan, NJ: Revell, 1978.

Schoenberg, Bernard, et al., eds. *Bereavement: Its Psychosocial Aspects.* New York: Columbia University, 1975.

Shelp, Earl E. and Ronald Sunderland, eds. *A Biblical Basis for Ministry.* Philadelphia: Westminster, 1981.

Southard, Samuel. *Pastoral Authority in Personal Relationships.* Nashville: Abingdon, 1969.

Stitzinger, James F. "Pastoral Ministry in History." In *Rediscovering Pastoral Ministry,* edited by John A. MacArthur, Jr. Dallas: Word, 1995.

Stone, Howard W. *The Word of God and Pastoral Care.* Nashville: Abingdon, 1988.

Switzer, David K. *The Minister as Crisis Counselor.* Nashville: Abingdon, 1974.

Thornton, Edward E. *Professional Education for Ministry.* Nashville: Abingdon, 1970.

Tournier, Paul. *Creative Suffering.* San Francisco: Harper and Row, 1981.

Vaughn, Ruth. *My God! My God! Answers to Our Anguished Cries.* Nashville: Impact, 1982.

Ver Straten, Charles A. *A Caring Church.* Grand Rapids: Baker Books, 1988.

Vining, John K., ed. *The Spirit of the Lord Is Upon Me: Essential Papers on Spirit-Filled Caregiving.* East Rockaway, NY: Cummings and Hathaway, 1997.

Vining, John K. and Edward E. Decker, eds. *Soul Care: A Pentecostal/Charismatic Perspective.* East Rockaway, NY: Cummings and Hathaway, 1996.

Weatherhead, Leslie D. *Why Do Men Suffer?* New York: Abingdon, 1936.

Weber, George W. *Today's Church: A Community of Exiles and Pilgrims.* Nashville: Abingdon, 1979.

Welu, Thomas C. "Pathological Bereavement: A Plan for Its Prevention." In *Bereavement: Its Psychosocial Aspects,* edited by Bernard Schoenberg, et al. New York: Columbia University, 1975.

Williams, Daniel D. *The Ministry and the Care of Souls.* New York: Harper and Row, 1961.

Yancey, Philip. *Where Is God When It Hurts?* Grand Rapids: Zondervan, 1977.

Index

Brock, Raymond, 20, 71
Bucer, Martin, 13
Bunyon, John, 16
Buttrick, George, 108, 109

Cabot, Richard, 19
Calvin, John, 10, 12, 13
Capp, Donald, 82
Carkhuff, Robert, 64, 126
Cathari, 10
Chaplaincy for Full Gospel Churches, 21
Characteristics of caregivers, 46
Charisma, 24
Charismatic worship, 122
Chronic suffering, 68
Chronos, 131
Chrysostom, John, 3
Church of God Theological Seminary, 24
City of Faith, 23, 24
Clebsch, W.A., 15, 16, 17, 33
Clement of Alexandria, 5, 6
Clinebell, Howard, 62, 63, 66
Clinical Pastoral Education, 19, 20, 58, 123
Coalition of Spirit-filled Churches, 21
College of Chaplains, 19, 23, 24
Comforting, 62, 65, **67**, 68
Communicating, 32, 45, 52
Congruence, 4, **59**, 60, 126
Craftsmanship, 34
Crick, Robert, 20, 21
Cyprian, 3

Decker, Edward E., 24, 25
Diakonia, 12, 37, 133
Dicks, Russell L., 19
Discerner, 7
Discernment, 7, 39, **49**, 50, 74, 75
Discipleship, 16, 17, 34, 41
Dobbins, Richard, 20, 24, 71

Edwards, Jonathan, 14
Egan, Gerard, 64
Emerge Ministries, 20

Roberts, Oral, 23, 41
Rogers, Carl, 58-65, 70, 124, 126

Salsbery, William, 14
Salvation Army, 16
Sattler, Michael, 13
Schaeffer, Edith, 111, 112
Serious mental illness, 83, 87
Sermons, 52
Servant and protector, 12
Shepherd, shepherding, 1, **2**, 3, 4, 15, 27, 28, 37, 43, 46, 122, 124
Southard, Samuel, 33, 34
Spiritual assessment, 74, 79, **88, 89**
Spiritual discernment, 7
Spurgeon, Charles, 15
Stages of life, 75
Steely, John, 101
Stitzinger, James F., 13, 15
Stone, Howard, 54, 65
Supportive community, 5
Sustaining, 15, 16, 17, 32, 33, 129
Switzer, David, 69

Tertullian, 4, 9
Thematic history, 15
Theologian, **7,** 37, 107
Theological presuppositions, 40
Therapist, **7**, 58, 59, 63
Third-Wavers, 20
Thomas, John R., 19
Thornton, Edward E., 19
Tillich, Paul, 63
Tournier, Paul, 112, 113
Trained pastor, 3, 22
Tyndale, William, 10

Understanding, 6, 12, 18, 29, 30, 35, 38, 47, 49, 51, 59, 63, 64, 65, **66**, 67, 68, 76, 79, 80, 93, 101, 105, 109, 118, 128
Unresolved grief, 68, 69

Vaughn, Ruth, 115, 116, 117, 118
Ver Straten, Charles, 2
Vining, John K., 22, 24, 25

Back Cover Insert

Are you confident in the care you give to hurting people?

This book by an experienced pastor and hospital chaplain will help you:

- Develop your caring skills

- Bring healing to people in pain

- Enhance your God-given gifts for caregiving

- Experience new success in helping people become whole

In *Ministry Between Miracles,* Spirit-filled pastors, counselors, and lay caregivers will find fresh perspectives on:

- Biblical concepts of pastoral care

- Avoiding dangerous mistakes

- How to move in the power of the Holy Spirit to bring new spiritual freedom

We must practice Spirit-led caregiving with maximum integrity. We must prepare ourselves through proper training to do skillful caregiving, and then surrender those skills to the Master.

LaVergne, TN USA
16 December 2009
167274LV00003B/22/A